THE AUTOMOBILE GIRLS AT WASHINGTON; OR, CHECKMATING THE PLOTS OF FOREIGN SPIES
BY
Laura Dent Crane

THE AUTOMOBILE GIRLS AT WASHINGTON; OR, CHECKMATING THE PLOTS OF FOREIGN SPIES

Published by Epic House Publishers

New York City, NY

First published circa 2015

Copyright © Epic House Publishers, 2015

All rights reserved

Except in the United States of America, this book is sold subject to the condition that it shall not, by way of trade or otherwise, be lent, re-sold, hired out, or otherwise circulated without the publisher's prior consent in any form of binding or cover other than that in which it is published and without a similar condition including this condition being imposed on the subsequent purchaser.

ABOUT EPIC HOUSE PUBLISHERS

Few things get the adrenaline going like fast-paced action, and with that in mind, **Epic House Publishers** can give readers the world's best action and adventure novels and stories in the click of a button, whether it's Tarzan on land or Moby Dick in the sea.

CHAPTER I

Barbara Thurston stood at the window of a large old-fashioned house, looking out into Connecticut Avenue. It was almost dark. An occasional light twinkled outside in the street, but the room in which Barbara was stationed was still shrouded in twilight.

Suddenly she heard a curtain at the farther end of the drawing-room rustle faintly.

Bab turned and saw a young man standing between the curtains, peering into the shadows with a pair of near-sighted eyes.

Barbara started. The stranger had entered the room through a small study that adjoined it. He seemed totally unaware of any other presence, for he was whistling softly: "Kathleen Mavourneen."

"I beg your pardon," Bab began impulsively, "but are you looking for some one?"

The newcomer flashed a charming smile at Barbara. He did not seem in the least surprised at her appearance.

"No," he declared cheerfully, "I was not looking for any one or anything. The butler told me Mr. Hamlin and Harriet were both out. But, I say, don't you think I am fortunate to have found you quite by accident! I came in here to loaf a few minutes."

Barbara frowned slightly. The young man's manner was surprisingly familiar, and she had never seen him before in her life.

"I hope I am not disturbing you," he went on gayly. "I am an attaché of the Russian legation, and a friend of Miss Hamlin's. I came with a message for Mr. Hamlin. I was wondering if it were worth while to wait for him. But I can go away if I am troublesome."

"Oh, no, you are not disturbing me in the least," Barbara returned. "I expect Miss Hamlin and my friends soon. We arrived in Washington last night, and the other girls have gone out to a reception. I had a headache and stayed at home. Won't you be seated while I ring for the butler to turn on the lights?"

The newcomer sat down, gravely watching Barbara.

"Would you like me to guess who you are?" he asked, after half a minute's silence.

Bab laughed. "I am sure you will give me the first chance to tell you your name. I did not recognize you at first. But I believe Harriet told us about you last night. She described several of her Washington friends to us. You are Peter Dillon, aren't you?"

"At your service," declared the young attaché, who looked almost boyish. "But now give me my opportunity. I do not know your name, but I have guessed this much. You are an 'Automobile Girl!' Permit me to bid you welcome to Washington."

Barbara nodded her head decidedly. "Yes, I am Barbara Thurston, one of the 'Automobile Girls.' There are four of us. Harriet has probably explained to you. My sister, Mollie Thurston, Grace Carter, Ruth Stuart and I form the quartet. Mr. William Hamlin is Ruth's uncle. So we are going to spend a few weeks here with Harriet and see the Capital. I have never been in Washington before."

"Then you have a new world before you, Miss Thurston," said the young man, his manner changing. "Washington is like no other city in the world, I think. I have been here for four years. Before that time I had lived in Dublin, in Paris, in St. Petersburg."

"Then you are not an American!" exclaimed Bab, regarding the young man with interest.

"I am a man without a country, Miss Thurston." Bab's visitor laughed carelessly. "Or, perhaps, I had better say I am a man of several countries. My father was an Irishman and a soldier of fortune. My mother was a Russian. Therefore, I am a member of the Russian legation in Washington in spite of my half-Irish name. Have you ever been abroad?"

"Oh, no," Bab returned, shaking her head. "For the past two years, since I have known Ruth Stuart, the 'Automobile Girls' have traveled about in this country a good deal. But we are only school girls still. We have never really made our début in society, although we mean to forget this while we are in Washington, and to see as much of the world as we can. I do wish I knew something about politics. It would make our visit in Washington so much more interesting."

"It is the most interesting game in the world," declared Barbara's companion, dropping for an instant his expression of indifference. His blue eyes flashed. Then he said quickly: "Perhaps you will let me teach you something of the political game at Washington. I am sure you will be quick to learn and to enjoy it."

"Thank you," Bab answered shyly. "But I am much too stupid ever to understand."

"I don't quite believe that. You know, you will, of course, hear a great deal about politics while you are the guests of the Assistant Secretary of State. Mr. Hamlin is one of the cleverest men in Washington. I am sure you will be instructing me in diplomacy by the end of a week. But good-bye; I must not keep you any longer. Will you tell Mr. Hamlin that I left the bundle of papers he desired on his study table? And please tell Harriet that I shall hope to be invited very often to see the 'Automobile Girls.'"

The young man looked intently at Barbara, as though trying to read her very thoughts while she returned his scrutiny with steady eyes. Then with a courteous bow, he left the room.

When Barbara found herself alone she returned to the window.

"I do wish the girls would come," she murmured to herself. "I am just dying to know what Mollie and Grace think of their first reception in Washington. Of course, Ruth has visited Harriet before, so the experience is not new to her. I am sorry I did not go with the girls, in spite of my headache. I wonder if some one is coming in here again! I seem to be giving a reception here myself."

By this time the room was lighted, and Barbara saw a young woman of about twenty-five years of age walk into the drawing-room and drop into a big arm chair with a little tired sigh.

"You are Miss Thurston, aren't you?" she asked briskly as Bab came forward to speak to her, wondering how on earth this newcomer knew her name and what could be the reason for this unexpected call.

"Yes," Barbara returned in a puzzled tone, "I am Miss Thurston."

"Oh, don't be surprised at my knowing your name," Bab's latest caller went on. "It is my business to know everybody. I met Mr. Dillon on the corner. He told me Harriet Hamlin was not at home and that I had better not come here this afternoon. I did not believe him; still I am not sorry Miss Hamlin is out, I would ever so much rather see you. Harriet Hamlin is dreadfully proud, and she is not a bit sympathetic. Do you think so?"

Bab was lost in wonder. What on earth could this talkative young woman wish of her? Did her visitor believe Bab would confide her opinion of Harriet to a complete stranger? But the young woman did not wait for an answer.

"I want to see you about something awfully important," she went on. "Please promise me you will do what I ask you before I tell you what it is."

Bab laughed. "Don't ask me that. Why you may be an anarchist, for all I know."

The new girl shook her head, smiling. She looked less tired now. She was pretty and fragile, with fair hair and blue eyes. She was very pale and was rather shabbily and carelessly dressed.

"No; I am not an anarchist," she said slowly. "I am a newspaper woman, which is almost as bad in some people's eyes, I suppose, considering the way society people fight against giving me news of themselves and their doings. I came to ask you if you would give me the pictures of the 'Automobile Girls' for my paper? Oh, you need not look so surprised. We have all heard of the 'Automobile Girls.' Everybody in Washington of importance has heard of you. Couldn't you let me write a sketch about you and your adventures, and put your photographs on the society page of our Sunday edition? It would be such a favor to me."

Barbara looked distressed. She was beginning to like her visitor. Though Barbara had been associated mainly with wealthy people in the last two years of the "Automobile Girls'" adventures, she could not help feeling interested in a girl who was evidently trying to make her own way in the world.

"I am awfully sorry," Bab declared almost regretfully, but before she finished speaking the drawing-room door opened and Ruth Stuart and Harriet Hamlin entered the room together.

"How is your head, Bab, dear?" Ruth cried, before she espied their caller.

Harriet Hamlin bowed coldly to the newspaper woman in the big arm chair. The young woman had flushed, looked uncomfortable at sight of Harriet and said almost humbly:

"I am sorry to interrupt you, Miss Hamlin, but my paper sent me to ask you for the pictures of your guests. May I have them?"

"Most certainly not, Miss Moore," Harriet answered scornfully. "My friends would not dream of allowing you to publish their pictures. And my father would not consent to it either. Just because he is Assistant Secretary of State I do not see why my visitors should be annoyed in this way. I hope you don't mind, Ruth and Barbara." Harriet's voice changed when she turned to address her cousin and friend. "Forgive my refusing Miss Moore for you. But it is out of the question."

Ruth and Bab both silently agreed with Harriet. But Barbara could not help feeling sorry for the other girl, who flushed painfully at Harriet's tone and turned to go without another word.

Bab followed the girl out into the hall.

"I am so sorry not to give you our photographs," Barbara declared. "But, of course, we cannot let you have them if Mr. Hamlin would object. And, to tell you the honest truth, the 'Automobile

Girls' would not like it either." Barbara smiled in such a frank friendly way that no one could have been vexed with her.

The older girl's eyes were full of tears, which she bravely winked out of sight.

"Everyone has his picture published in the papers nowadays," she replied.

"I am sure I intended no discourtesy to you or to Miss Hamlin."

Then the girl's self-control gave way. She was very tired, and Bab's sympathy unnerved her. "I hate Harriet Hamlin," she whispered, passionately. "I am as well bred as she is. Because I am poor, and have to support my mother, is no reason why she should treat me as though I were dust under her feet. I shall have a chance to get even with her, some day, just as certainly as I live. Then, won't I take my revenge!"

Barbara did not know what to reply, so she went on talking quietly. "I am sure your asking us for our pictures was a very great compliment to us. Only important people and beauties and belles have their pictures in the society papers. It is just because the 'Automobile Girls' are too insignificant to be shown such an honor that we can't consent. But please don't be angry with us. I am sure Harriet did not intend to wound your feelings, and I hope I shall see you soon again."

Marjorie Moore shook Barbara's hand impulsively before she went out into the gathering darkness. "I like you," she said warmly. "I wish we might be friends. Good-night."

"Where are Mollie and Grace?" was Bab's first question when she rejoined Ruth and Harriet.

"They would not come away from the reception," Harriet returned, smiling. She was quite unconscious of having treated Marjorie Moore unkindly. "Ruth and I were worried about your headache, so we did not wish to leave you alone any longer. Strange to relate, Father offered to stay until Mollie and Grace were ready to come home. That is a great concession on his part, as he usually runs away from a reception at the first opportunity that offers itself. Mrs. Wilson, a friend of Father's is helping him to look after Mollie and Grace this afternoon. Bab, did some boxes come for me this afternoon? I left orders at the shop to send them when Father would surely be out. Come on upstairs, children, and see my new finery."

"Why, Harriet, are you getting more clothes?" Ruth exclaimed. "You are like 'Miss Flora McFlimsey, of Madison Square, who never had anything good enough to wear.'"

"I am no such thing, Ruth Stuart," returned her cousin, a little peevishly. "You don't understand. Does she, Barbara? Ruth has so much money she simply cannot realize what it means to try to make a good appearance on a small allowance, especially here in Washington where one goes out so much."

"I was only joking, Harriet," Ruth apologized as she and Barbara obediently followed their hostess upstairs. Bab, however, secretly wondered how she and Mollie were to manage in Washington, with their simple wardrobes, if their young hostess thought that clothes were the all-important thing in Washington society.

Harriet Hamlin was twenty years of age, but she seemed much older to Bab and Ruth. In the first place, Harriet was an entirely different type of girl. She had been mistress of her father's house in Washington since she was sixteen. She had received her father's guests and entertained his friends; and at eighteen she had made her début into Washington society, and had taken her position as one of the women of the Cabinet. Harriet's mother, Ruth's aunt, had died a few months before Mr. Hamlin had received his appointment as Assistant Secretary of State. Since that time Harriet had borne the responsibilities of a grown woman, and being an only child she had to a certain extent done as she pleased, although she was secretly afraid of her cold, dignified father.

Mr. William Hamlin was one of the ablest men in Washington. He was a quiet, stern, reserved man, and although he was proud of his daughter, of her beauty and accomplishments, he was also very strict with her. He was a poor man, and it was hard work for Harriet to keep up the appearance necessary to her father's position on his salary as Assistant Secretary of State. Harriet, however, never dared tell her father of this, and Mr. Hamlin never offered Harriet either sympathy or advice.

Barbara and Ruth could only watch with admiring eyes and little exclamations of delight the exquisite garments that Harriet now lifted out of three big, pasteboard boxes; a beautiful yellow crêpe frock, a pale green satin evening gown and a gray broadcloth tailor-made suit. Harriet was tall and dark, with very black hair and large dark eyes. She was considered one of the beauties of the "younger set" in Washington society. Ruth had not seen her cousin for several years, until she received the invitation to bring the "Automobile Girls" to Washington.

Ruth Stuart and Barbara Thurston had changed very little since their last outing together at Palm Beach. Barbara was now nearly eighteen. At the close of the school year she was to be graduated from the Kingsbridge High School. And she hoped to be able to enter Vassar College the following fall. Yet the fact that she was in Washington early in December requires an explanation.

Two weeks before Bab had walked slowly home to Laurel Cottage at about three o'clock one November afternoon with a great pile of books under her arm.

On the front porch of their little cottage she found her mother and

Mollie, greatly excited. A telegram had just come from Ruth Stuart. The

"Automobile Girls" were invited to visit Ruth's cousin in Washington,

D.C. Ruth wished them to start at the end of the week.

Bab's face flushed with pleasure at the news. She had not been with her beloved Ruth since the Easter before. Then the color died out of her face and her cheeks showed an unaccustomed pallor.

"I am so sorry, Mother," Bab responded. "I would give anything in the world to see Ruth. But I simply can't stop school just now, or I shall lose the scholarship. Mollie, you can accept Ruth's invitation. You and Grace Carter can go to Washington together. You won't mind going without me."

"I shall not stir a single step without you," blue-eyed Mollie returned firmly. "And Mother thinks you can go!"

Mollie and Mrs. Thurston, aided by Bab's teachers, at last persuaded Barbara to take a few weeks' holiday. Bab could study to make up for lost time during the Christmas holidays. For no one, except the young woman herself, doubted Barbara's ability to win the desired Vassar scholarship.

And so it was arranged that Bab and Mollie should go with Ruth to Washington. Bab had grown taller and more slender in the past few months. Her brown braids are now always coiled about her graceful head. Her hair was parted in the middle, although a few little curls still escaped in the old, careless fashion.

Ruth Stuart, too, was looking sweeter and fresher than ever, and was the same ingenuous, unspoiled girl, whose sunny disposition no amount of wealth and fashion could change.

Readers of the first volume in the "Automobile Girls Series," entitled "The Automobile Girls At Newport," will recall how, nearly two years ago, Ruth Stuart, with her father and her aunt, Miss Sallie Stuart, came from their home in far away Chicago to spend the summer in Kingsbridge, New Jersey. The day that Barbara Thurston stopped a pair of runaway horses and saved Ruth Stuart from death she did not dream that she had turned the first page in the history of the "Automobile Girls." A warm friendship sprang up between Ruth and Bab, and a little later Ruth Stuart invited Barbara, her younger sister, Mollie Thurston, and their friend, Grace Carter, to take a trip to Newport in her own, red automobile with Ruth herself as chauffeur and her aunt, Miss Sallie Stuart, as chaperon.

Exciting days at Newport followed, and the four girls brought to bay the "Boy Raffles," the cracksman, who had puzzled the fashionable world! There were many thrilling adventures connected with the discovery of this "society thief," and the "Automobile Girls" proved themselves capable of meeting whatever emergencies sprang up in their path.

In "The Automobile Girls in the Berkshires," the second volume of the "Automobile Girls Series," the scene is laid in a little log cabin on top of one of the highest peaks in the Berkshire hills, where the four girls and Miss Sallie spent a happy period of time "roughing it." There it was that they discovered an Indian Princess and laid the "Ghost of Lost Man's Trail."

In the third volume of the series, "The Automobile Girls Along the Hudson," the quartet of youthful travelers, accompanied by Miss Sallie Stuart, motored through the beautiful Sleepy Hollow country, spending several weeks at the home of Major Ted Eyck, an old friend of the Stuarts. There many diverting experiences fell to their lot, and before leaving the hospitable major's home they were instrumental in saving it from destruction by forest fires.

The fourth volume of the series, "The Automobile Girls at Chicago," relates the adventures of the four friends during the Christmas holidays, which Mollie, Grace and Bab spent with Ruth at Chicago and at "Treasureholme," the country estate of the Presbys, who were cousins of the Stuart family. While there, principally through the cleverness of Barbara Thurston, the hiding place of a rich treasure buried by one of The ancestors of the Presbys was discovered in time to prevent the financial ruin of both Richard Presby and Robert Stuart, who had become deeply involved through speculation in wheat.

Before Mollie, Grace and Barbara returned to Kingsbridge, Mr. Stuart had promised that they should see Ruth again in March at Palm Beach, where he had planned a happy reunion for the "Automobile Girls." There it was that they had, through a series of happenings, formed the acquaintance of a mysterious countess and become involved in the net of circumstances that was woven about her. How they continued to be her friend in spite of dark rumors afloat to the effect that she was an impostor and how she afterwards turned out to be a princess, is fully set forth in "The Automobile Girls at Palm Beach."

"Really, Bab," said Ruth, as the two girls went upstairs to their rooms to dress for dinner, "I have not had a chance to talk to you, alone, since we arrived in Washington. How is your mother?"

"As well as can be," Bab answered. "How is darling Aunt Sallie? I am so sorry she did not come to Washington with you to chaperon us. There is no telling what mischief we may get into without her."

Ruth laughed. "I have special instructions for the 'Automobile Girls' from Aunt Sallie. We are to be particularly careful to mind our 'P's' and 'Q's' on this visit, for Aunt Sallie wishes us to make a good impression in Washington."

Barbara sighed. "I'll try, Ruth," she declared, "but you know what remarkable talent I have for getting into mischief."

"Then you are to be specially par-tic-u-lar, Mistress Bab!" Ruth said teasingly. "For Aunt Sallie's last words to me were: 'Tell Barbara she is to look before she leaps.'"

Barbara shook her brown head vigorously. "I am not the impetuous Bab of other automobile days. But, just the same, I wish Aunt Sallie had come along with you."

"Oh, she may join us later," Ruth returned. "To tell you the truth, Bab, Aunt Sallie is not fond of Harriet. She thinks Harriet is clever and pretty, but vain and spoiled. Here come Mollie and Grace. Home from that reception at last!"

The other two girls burst into Ruth's room at this moment.

"Whom do you think we have seen?" called out Miss Mollie rapturously. "Oh, Washington is the greatest fun! I feel just like a girl in a book, we have been presented to so many noted people. I tell you, Barbara Thurston, we are country girls no longer! Now we have been traveling about the country so much with Ruth and Mr. Stuart, that we know people everywhere. Just guess whom we know in Washington?"

"I can guess," Ruth rejoined, clapping her hands. "You have seen Mrs.

Post and Hugh. Surely, you had not forgotten that they live in

Washington. Hugh has finished college and has a position in the Forestry

Department. I had a note from him this morning."

"And didn't tell! Oh, Ruth!" teased Grace Carter. "But, Bab, what about our Lenox friends, who spend their winters in Washington?"

"You mean Dorothy and Gwendolin Morton, the British Ambassador's daughters, and funny little Franz Haller, the German secretary, I hope we shall see them. But do hurry, children. Please don't keep the Assistant Secretary of State waiting for his dinner. That would surely be a bad beginning for our Washington visit. No, Mollie Thurston; don't you put on your very best dress for dinner to-night. I have just gotten out your white muslin."

"But Harriet wears such lovely clothes all the time, Bab," Mollie pleaded, when she and

Barbara were alone.

"Never mind, child. Harriet Hamlin is not Mollie Thurston," Barbara concluded wisely.

CHAPTER II

It was Harriet Hamlin's reception day. There are certain times appointed in Washington when the members of the President's Cabinet hold receptions.

The "Automobile Girls" had come to Washington in time for one of these special entertainments. For, as Harriet explained, they could see everyone worth seeing at once. Not only would the diplomats, the senators and congressmen call with their wives, but the Army and Navy officers, all official Washington would appear to pay their respects to Mr. William Hamlin and his lovely daughter.

"Then there will be a crowd of unimportant people besides," Harriet had continued. "People who are never asked to any small parties come to this reception just because they can get in. So you girls will have to entertain yourselves this morning. I have a thousand things to do. Why not take the girls to look at the White House, Ruth? That is the first thing to do in Washington. I am sorry I can't go with you. But you just walk straight down Connecticut Avenue and you can't miss it."

It was a perfect day. Although it was early in December, the atmosphere was like Indian summer. Washington shone sparkling white through a dim veil of haze. The "Automobile Girls" walked briskly along toward the White House, chatting every step of the way.

"Where are the poplar trees planted along this avenue by Thomas Jefferson, Ruth?" Grace Carter demanded. "I read somewhere that Jefferson meant to make this avenue look like the famous street called 'Unter den Linden' in Berlin."

"He did, child, but most of the poplar trees died," Ruth rejoined, "and some one else planted these oaks and elms. Why are you so silent, Barbara? Are you tired?"

"I think Washington is the most beautiful city in the whole world," Bab answered with sudden enthusiasm.

"Wait until you have seen it," Ruth teased. "Uncle William wants to take us through the Capitol. But I suppose there is no harm in our looking at the outside of the White House. Later on, when we go to one of the President's receptions, we can see the inside of it."

"Shall we ever see the President?" Mollie asked breathlessly. "Won't it be wonderful? I never dreamed that even Mr. Hamlin could take us to the President's home."

"Here we are at the White House," said Ruth.

The "Automobile Girls" stood silent for a moment, looking in through the autumn foliage at the simple colonial mansion, which is the historic "White House."

"I am glad our White House looks like that," Bab said, after half a moment's pause. "I was so afraid it would be pretentious. But it is just big and simple and dignified as our President's home ought to be. It makes me feel so glad to be an American," Barbara ended with a flush. She was afraid the other girls were laughing at her.

"I think so too, Bab," Ruth agreed. "I don't see why girls cannot be as patriotic as boys. We may be able to serve our country in some way, some day. I hope we shall have the chance."

The "Automobile Girls" had entered the White House grounds and were strolling along through the park.

Bab and Ruth were talking of the beauties of Washington. But no such thoughts were engrossing pretty Mollie's attention. Mollie's mind was dwelling on the society pleasures the "Automobile Girls" expected to enjoy at the Capital City. Grace Carter was listening to Barbara's and Ruth's animated conversation.

From the very first days at Newport, Mollie Thurston had cared more for society than had her sister and two friends. Her dainty beauty and pretty manners made her a favorite wherever she went. Mollie's friends had spoiled her, and since her arrival in Washington the old story had repeated itself. Harriet Hamlin had already taken Mollie under her special protection. And Mollie was wildly excited with the thought of the social experiences ahead of her.

The four girls spent some time strolling about the White House grounds. Then Ruth proposed that they take a car and visit the Congressional Library.

"I think it is the most beautiful building in Washington, and, in fact, one of the finest in the world," she said enthusiastically, and later when the "Automobile Girls" were fairly inside the famous library, they fully agreed with her. It was particularly hard to tear Barbara away from what seemed to her the most fascinating place she was ever in, and she announced her intention of visiting it again at the first opportunity.

The sightseers arrived home in time for luncheon and at four o'clock that afternoon they stood in a row, beside Harriet Hamlin and her father, helping to receive the guests who crowded in to the reception. Some of the women wore beautiful gowns, others looked as though they had come from small towns where the residents knew nothing of fashionable society.

Mollie and Bab wore the white chiffon frocks Mr. Prescott had presented them with in Chicago. But Grace and Ruth wore gowns that had been ordered for this particular occasion. Bab thought their white frocks, which looked as though they were new, as pretty as any of the gowns worn there. But little Mollie was not satisfied. She hated old clothes, no matter how well they looked. And Harriet Hamlin was rarely beautiful in an imported gown of pale, yellow crêpe.

After receiving for an hour, Bab slipped quietly into a chair near a window. She wished to examine the guests at her leisure. Mollie and Ruth were deep in conversation with Mrs. Post and Hugh. Grace was talking to Dorothy and Gwendolin Morton.

Barbara's eyes wandered eagerly over the throng of people. Suddenly some one touched her on the shoulder.

"You do not remember me, do you?"

Bab turned and saw a young woman.

"I am Marjorie Moore," said the newcomer. "I am the girl who came to ask you for your pictures. Perhaps you think it is strange for me to come to Harriet Hamlin's reception when she was so rude to me last night. But I am not a guest. Besides, newspaper people are not expected to have any feelings. My newspaper sent me to find out what people were here this afternoon. So here I am! I know everybody in Washington. Would you like me to point out some of the celebrities to you? See that stunning woman just coming in at the door? She has the reputation of being the most popular woman in Washington. But nobody knows just where she comes from, or who she is, or how she gets her money. But I must not talk Washington gossip. You'll meet her soon yourself."

"How do you do, Miss Moore?" broke in a charming contralto voice. "You are the very person I wish to see. I can give you some news for your paper. It is not very important, but I thought you might like to have it."

"You are awfully good, Mrs. Wilson," Marjorie Moore replied gratefully. "I have just been talking to Miss Thurston about you. May I introduce her? She has just arrived in Washington, and I told her, only half a second ago, that you were the nicest woman in this town."

Mrs. Wilson laughed quietly. "I know Miss Thurston's sister and her friend, Miss Carter. Mr. Hamlin let me help chaperon them at a reception yesterday afternoon. But Miss Moore has been flattering me dreadfully. I am a very unimportant person, though I happen to have the good fortune to be a friend of Mr. Hamlin's and Harriet's. I am keeping house in Washington at present. Some day you must come to see me."

Bab thanked her new acquaintance. She thought she had never seen a more unusual looking woman. It was impossible to guess her age. Mrs. Wilson's hair was snow-white, but her face was as young as a girl's and her eyes were fascinatingly dark under her narrow penciled brows. She was gowned in a pale blue broadcloth dress, and wore on her head a large black hat trimmed with a magnificent black plume.

"The top of the afternoon to you!" declared a new arrival in Bab's sheltered corner. "How is a man to find you if you will hide behind curtains?" This time Bab recognized Peter Dillon, her acquaintance of the afternoon before.

Mrs. Wilson, whose manner suggested a charming frankness and innocence, took Peter by the arm. "Which of the three Graces do you mean to devote yourself to this afternoon, Peter? You shall not flatter us all at once."

"I flatter?" protested Peter, in aggrieved tones. "Why truthfulness is my strong point."

Marjorie Moore gave a jarring laugh. "Is it, Mr. Dillon?" she returned, not too politely. "Please count me out of Mr. Dillon's flatteries. He does not include a woman who works in them." Marjorie Moore hurried away.

"Whew-w!" ejaculated Peter. "Miss Moore does not love me, does she? I came up only to say a few words. Miss Hamlin is keeping me busy this afternoon. Come and have some coffee, Miss Thurston. I am sure you look tired."

"I would rather not," Barbara protested. "I am going to run away upstairs for a minute, if you will excuse me."

Before Barbara could make her escape from the drawing-room she saw that Peter Dillon and Mrs. Wilson had both lost their frivolous manner and were deep in earnest conversation.

CHAPTER III

Bab knew that at the rear of this floor of Mr. Hamlin's house there was a small room that was seldom used. She hoped to find refuge in it for a few minutes, and then to return to her friends.

The room was empty. Bab sank down into a great arm chair and closed her eyes.

A few moments later she opened them though she heard no sound. A fat little Chinese gentleman stood regarding her with an expression of amusement on his face.

Barbara jumped hastily to her feet. Where was she? She felt frightened. Although the man before her was yellow and foreign, and wore strange Chinese clothes, he was evidently a person of importance. Had Barbara awakened at the Court of Pekin? Her companion wore a loose, black satin coat, heavily embroidered in flowers and dragons and a round, close fitting silk cap with a button on top of it.

"I beg your pardon," Bab exclaimed in confusion. "Whom did you wish to see? There is no one in here."

The Chinese gentleman made Bab a stately bow. "No one," he protested. "This is the first time, since my residence in America, that I have heard an American girl speak of herself as no one. Miss United States is always some one in her own country. But may I therefore present myself to little 'Miss No One'? I am Dr. Tu Fang Wu, His Imperial Chinese Majesty's Envoy Extraordinary and Minister Plenipotentiary to the United States."

"I am very proud to meet you, Mr. Minister," Barbara returned, wondering if "Mr. Minister" was the proper way to address a foreign ambassador. She thought Mr. Hamlin had told her so, only the night before.

Bab did not know in the least what she should do or say to such a distinguished Oriental. She might make a mistake at any minute. For Bab had been learning, every hour since her arrival in Washington, that in no place is social etiquette more important than in the Capital City.

"May I find Mr. Hamlin for you?" Bab suggested, hoping to make her escape.

The Chinese Minister shook his head slowly. "Mr. Hamlin is engaged with his other guests."

"Then won't you be seated?" Bab asked in desperation. Really she and this strange yellow gentleman could not stand staring at each other the whole afternoon. It made Bab feel creepy to have a Chinaman regard her so steadfastly and without the slightest change of expression, even if he were a foreign minister.

Bab felt this meeting to be one of the strangest experiences of her whole life. She had never seen a Chinaman before, except on the street carrying a basket of laundry. But here she was forced into a tête-à-tête with one in the highest social position.

"Have you any daughters?" Barbara asked in her effort to break the awful silence.

Mr. Tu Fang Wu again bowed gravely. "I have one daughter and one small son. My daughter is not here with me this afternoon. Chinese girls do not go to entertainments where there are young men. My daughter has been brought up according to the customs of our country. But she has been in Washington for several years. I fear she, too, would like to be emancipated, like the American girl. It is not possible, although she enjoys many privileges she will not have when she returns to China. My daughter is betrothed to a nobleman in her own country. Perhaps you would like to meet my daughter, Wee Tu? She is fifteen years old. I shall ask Miss Hamlin to bring you to luncheon at the Embassy."

To Barbara's relief Mr. William Hamlin now appeared at the door.

The Chinese minister again bowed profoundly to Barbara. "I was looking for your smoking-room," he laughed, "but I found this young woman instead."

As the two men went out of the room, Bab had difficulty in making sure that she had not been dreaming of this fat, yellow gentleman.

"Barbara Thurston, what do you mean by running away by yourself?" exclaimed Grace Carter, a moment later. "We have been looking for you for ten minutes."

Hugh Post, Mollie and a strange young man were close behind Grace.

"I want to present my friend, Lieutenant Elmer Wilson," Hugh announced.

"He is a very important person in Washington."

"Not a bit of it," laughed the young man. "I am one of the President's aides. I try to make myself generally useful."

"Your work must be very interesting," Barbara said quickly. "Do you—"

Just then a soft contralto voice interrupted her. "Are you ready to go with me, Elmer?" it said.

Barbara recognized the voice as belonging to the Mrs. Wilson whom she had met in the drawing room not an hour before. Could it be that this young and lovely looking woman was the mother of Elmer Wilson? Surely the young man was at least twenty-two years old.

"Coming in a moment, Mother," Elmer replied. "Have you said good-bye to Harriet?"

"Harriet is not in the reception room now. Nearly all her guests have gone," Mrs. Wilson murmured softly. "Mr. Hamlin is angry. But poor Harriet ought to have a chance to talk for a few minutes to the richest young man in Washington. I will leave you, Elmer. If you see Harriet, you may tell her I did not think it fair to disturb her."

Barbara went back to the drawing-room to search for Ruth. She found Ruth standing next her uncle, Mr. Hamlin, saying the adieux in Harriet's place. A few moments later the last visitor had withdrawn and Mr. Hamlin quickly left Ruth and Bab alone.

Mr. Hamlin was a small man, with iron gray hair, a square jaw and thin, tightly closed lips. He seldom talked, and the "Automobile Girls" felt secretly afraid of him.

"Uncle is dreadfully angry with Harriet," Ruth explained to Bab, after Mr. Hamlin was out of hearing. "But he is awfully strict and I do not think he is exactly fair. He does not give Harriet credit for what she does, but he gets awfully cross if she makes any mistakes. Harriet is upstairs, in her own sitting-room, talking to a great friend of hers. He is a man Uncle hates, although he has known Charlie Meyers since childhood. He is immensely rich, but he is very ill-bred, and that is why Uncle dislikes him. I don't think Harriet cares a bit more for this young man than she does for half a dozen others. But if Uncle doesn't look out Harriet will marry him for spite. Harriet hates being poor. She is not poor, really. But I am afraid she is terribly extravagant. Promise not to laugh when you see Charlie Meyers. He looks a little like a pig, he is so pink and fat."

"Girls!" called Harriet's voice. "Are you still in here? Mr. Meyers has just gone, and I wanted you to meet him. He is going to have a motor party and take you to see Mount Vernon. We can drive along the Potomac and have our supper somewhere in the country."

"I'm going to drive Mr. A. Bubble, Harriet," Ruth replied. "As long as I brought my car to Washington I must use it. But I suppose we can get up guests enough to fill two automobiles, can't we?"

"Where's Father?" Harriet inquired, trying to conceal a tremor in her voice. "Did he know I was upstairs?"

"I am afraid he did, Harriet," Ruth replied.

"Well, I don't care," declared Harriet defiantly. "I will select my own friends. Charlie Meyers is stupid and ill-bred, but he is good natured, and I am tired of position and poverty."

"You are no such thing, Harriet," protested Ruth, taking her cousin by the hand and leading her to a long mirror. "There, look at yourself in your yellow gown. You look like a queen. Please don't be silly."

"It's clothes that make the woman, Ruth," Harriet replied, kissing Ruth unexpectedly. "And this yellow gown is just one of the things that troubles me. Dear me, I am glad the reception is over!"

CHAPTER IV

"Shall we eat our luncheon with chopsticks to-day?" Mollie Thurston asked Harriet Hamlin an hour before the "Automobile Girls" and their hostess were to start for the Chinese Embassy.

Harriet laughed good-humoredly at Mollie's question. "You absurd child, don't you know the Chinese minister is one of the most cultivated men in Washington! When he is in America he does what the Americans do. But his wife, Lady Tu, is delightfully Chinese. She paints her face in the Chinese fashion and wears beautiful Chinese clothes in her own home. And the little Chinese daughter is a darling. Really, Mollie, you will feel as though you had been on a trip to the Orient when you meet dainty little Wee Tu."

"Oh, I don't believe a Chinese girl can be attractive," Mollie argued, her eyes fixed on the pile of pretty gowns which Harriet was laying out on her bed.

"Do wear the rose-colored gown to-day, Harriet!" Mollie pleaded. "It is such a love of a frock and so becoming to you with your white skin and dark hair. Dear me, it must be nice to have such lovely clothes!" Mollie paused for a minute.

Harriet turned around to find her little friend blushing.

"I do hope," Mollie went on, "that you are not going to feel ashamed of Bab and me while we are your guests in Washington. You can see for yourself that we are poor, and have only a few gowns. Of course it is different with Grace and Ruth. But our father is dead, and—" Mollie stopped. She did not know how to go on with her explanation. Somehow she did not feel that Barbara or her mother would approve of her apologizing to Harriet for their simple wardrobes.

"Mollie!" Harriet exclaimed reproachfully. "You know I think you and Barbara are so pretty and clever that it does not matter what your clothes are like. Besides, if you should ever want anything special to wear while you are here, why, I have a host of gowns."

Mollie shook her head. Of course she could not borrow Harriet's gowns. And, though Harriet was trying to comfort her, her tone showed very plainly that she had noticed the slimness of the Thurston girls' preparations in the matter of wardrobe for several weeks of gayety in Washington.

At a little before one o'clock the "Automobile Girls" and Harriet were ushered into the reception room of the Chinese Embassy by a grave Chinese servant clad in immaculate white and wearing his long pig-tail curled on top of his head.

The minister and his wife came forward. Lady Tu wore a dress of heavy Chinese embroidery with a long skirt and a short full coat. Her hair was inky black and built out on each side of her head. She had a band of gold across it and golden flowers set with jewels hung above each ear. Her face was enameled in white and a small patch of crimson was painted just under her lip.

Bab could hardly restrain an exclamation of delight at the beauty of the reception room. The walls were covered with Chinese silk and heavy panels of embroidery. A Chinese banner, with a great dragon on it, hung over the mantel-piece. The furniture was elaborately carved teakwood.

The girls at once glanced around for the Chinese minister's daughter. But she was no where to be seen. Instead, Peter Dillon, Bab's first chance acquaintance in Washington, was smiling a welcome. Mrs. Wilson and her son were also present. The two or three other visitors were unknown to the "Automobile Girls." Even when luncheon was served the little Chinese girl did not make her appearance. The four girls were beginning to feel rather disappointed. They had come to the Embassy chiefly to see Wee Tu, and they were evidently not going to be granted that pleasure.

Just as they were about to go back to the reception room, Mr. Tu Fang Wu suggested courteously to his girl guests: "If it pleases you, will you now go up to my daughter's apartments? She does not eat her meals with us when we entertain young men guests. It is not the custom of our country." The Chinese minister touched a bell and another Chinese servant appeared, his slippered feet making no noise. At the top of the stairs a Chinese woman met the "Automobile Girls" and conducted them to the apartment of Wee Tu, the minister's daughter.

Wee Tu bowed her head to the floor when the "Automobile Girls" entered. But when she raised her face her little black eyes were glowing, and a faint pink showed under her smooth, yellow skin. Think what it meant to this little Chinese maid, with her shut-in life, to meet four American girls like Barbara, Ruth, Grace and Mollie! Harriet had lingered behind for a few moments.

"Your most honorable presence does my miserable self much honor," stated Wee Tu automatically.

Bab laughed. She simply could not help it. Wee Tu's greeting seemed so absurd to her ears, though she knew it was the Chinese manner of speaking. But Bab's merry laugh saved the situation, as it often had done before, for the little Chinese maid laughed in return, and the five girls sat giggling in the most intimate fashion.

The servant passed around preserved Chinese fruits, nuts and dried melon seed.

"Is Miss Hamlin not with you?" the Chinese minister's daughter asked finally, in broken English.

At this moment Harriet's voice was heard in the corridor. She was talking gayly to Peter Dillon. The Chinese girl caught the sound of the young man's charming laugh. Bab was gazing straight at Wee Tu. Wee Tu looked like a beautiful Chinese doll, not a bit like a human being.

At the entrance to Wee Tu's apartment Peter bowed gracefully. He waited until Harriet entered.

"Your most honorable ladyship," he inquired. "Have I your permission to enter your divine apartment? Your most noble father has waived ceremony in my favor and says I may be allowed to see you in company with your other guests. You are to pretend you are an American girl to-day."

Wee Tu again made a low bow, almost touching the soft Chinese rug with her crown of black hair. Her mantle was of blue silk crepe embroidered in lotus flowers, and she wore artificial lotus blossoms drooping on either side of her head.

After Peter's entrance, Wee Tu did not speak nor smile. She sat with her slender yellow hands clasped together, her nails so long they were tipped with gold to prevent their breaking. Her tiny feet in their embroidered slippers looked much too small for walking.

Peter made himself agreeable to all the girls. He chatted with Harriet, joked with Bab and Ruth. Now and then he spoke to the Chinese girl in some simple gentle fashion that she could understand.

"Peter Dillon is awfully attractive," Bab thought. "I wonder why I was prejudiced against him at first because of what that newspaper girl said."

Peter walked with Barbara back to Mr. Hamlin's house.

"Would you mind my asking you a question?" Bab demanded when they were fairly on the way.

Peter laughed. "It's a woman's privilege, isn't it?"

"Well, how do you happen to be so intimate at the Chinese minister's?" was Barbara's direct question. "They seemed so formal and then all of a sudden Mr. Tu Fang Wu let you come up to see his daughter."

"I know them very well," Peter returned simply. "I often dine at the Chinese minister's with his family. So I have met his daughter several times before. I have made myself useful to Mr. Tu Fang Wu once or twice, and my legation likes me to keep in touch with the people in authority."

"Oh," exclaimed Barbara. She remembered that Peter was equally intimate at Mr. Hamlin's, and she wondered how he managed to keep up such a variety of acquaintances.

"I wonder if you would do a fellow a favor some day?" Peter asked. "I'll bet you have lots of nerve. Harriet is apt to get frightened at the critical minute."

"It would all depend on what you asked me to do," Bab returned puzzled by Peter's remark.

"Oh, I won't ask you until I have managed to do something for you first. It is only that I think you can see a joke and I have a good one that I mean to try some day," Peter replied.

CHAPTER V

The next morning, Peter Dillon was lounging in Mrs. Wilson's library, chatting with her on apparently easy terms.

"I think it is a special dispensation of Providence that sent the 'Automobile Girls' to Washington to visit Harriet Hamlin just at this particular time, Mrs. Wilson," declared Peter Dillon.

Mrs. Wilson walked back and forth across her drawing room floor several times before she answered. She looked older in the early morning light. But her restlessness did not disturb Peter, who was reclining gracefully in a chair, smoking a cigarette.

"I am not sure you have reason to bless Providence, Peter Dillon," Mrs. Wilson protested. "What a man you are! You simply cannot judge all girls by the same standard. Some day you are going to meet a girl who is cleverer than you are. And then, where will you be?"

"Oh, I'll go slowly," Peter argued. "I know I am taking chances in making friends with the clever one. But she has more nerve and courage than the others. I am sure it will be much better to leave Harriet out of the whole business, if possible."

"All right, Peter," Mrs. Wilson agreed. "Manage your own affairs, since this happens to be your own special joke. But you had much better have left the whole matter to me."

"And spoil my good time with five charming girls?" Peter protested, smiling. "No, Mrs. Wilson; that is too much to ask of me. If I can't carry the thing off successfully, you will come to the rescue and help me. You've promised that. We have had our little jokes together before. But this strikes me as being about the best of the whole lot. We will have everybody in Washington laughing up his sleeve pretty soon. There will be a few people who won't laugh, but so long as we keep quiet we need not worry about them. Has Elmer gone to work? I know I have made you a dreadfully early visit. It is very charming of you to be up in time to see me."

"Don't flatter me, Peter; it is not worth while," Mrs. Wilson said angrily. Then she smiled. "Never mind, Peter; you can no more help flattering than you can help breathing, whether your reason is a good or a bad one. I suppose it is because you are an Irishman. By the way, Elmer admires one of these charming 'Automobile Girls.' He has talked of no one else except Mollie Thurston since Harriet's tea. Be careful what you say or do before him."

"I shall be careful," Peter returned easily. "My attentions are directed toward the other sister. How have you managed to keep that big boy of yours so much in the dark about—oh, a number of things?" finished Peter.

"It is because Elmer has perfect faith in me, Peter," Mrs. Wilson answered, passing her hand over her eyes to hide their expression.

"As all other men have had before him, my lady," Peter avowed. "Is it true that Mr. William Hamlin is now a worshiper at your shrine?"

"Absurd!" protested Mrs. Wilson. "Here comes Elmer."

"Why, Peter Dillon, this is a surprise!" exclaimed the young lieutenant, walking into the room in search of his mother. "I never knew Mother to get up so early before. I have just been inquiring of your maid, Mother, to know what had become of you. Harriet Hamlin wants you to chaperon us on an automobile ride out to Mt. Vernon and along the Potomac River. Charlie Meyers is giving the party, and Harriet thinks her father won't object if you will go along to look after us. That Charlie Meyers is an awful bounder! But Harriet wants to show her little Yankee visitors the sights. Do come along with us, Mother. For I have a fancy I should like to stroll through the old Washington garden with 'sweet sixteen.'"

"I will chaperon you with pleasure, Elmer," Mrs. Wilson agreed. "But what about you, Peter? Are you not invited?"

Peter looked chagrined.

"No; I am not invited, and I call it unkind of Harriet. She knows I am dreadfully impressed with the 'Automobile Girls.'"

Mrs. Wilson and Elmer both laughed provokingly. "That is just what's the trouble with you, Peter. Harriet is accustomed to your devotion to her. Now that you have turned your thoughts in another direction, she may look upon you as a faithless swain," Mrs. Wilson teased.

"Don't undertake more than you can manage, Peter," teased Elmer Wilson.

"That is good advice for Peter. Remember, Peter, I have warned you. Some day you will run across a girl who is cleverer than you are. Then look out, young man," Mrs. Wilson repeated.

But Peter only laughed cheerfully. "What girl isn't cleverer than a man?" he protested. "Au revoir. I shall do my best to persuade Harriet to let me go along with her party this afternoon. I suppose we shall be starting soon after luncheon, as it is Saturday."

"Mother, can you let me have some money?" Elmer asked, as soon as Peter was out of hearing. "I am ashamed to ask you for it. But going out in society does cost a fellow an awful lot."

Mrs. Wilson shook her head. "I am sorry, Boy; I can't let you have anything just now. I am short of money myself at present. But I expect to have some money coming in, say in about two weeks, or even ten days. Then I can let you have what you like."

*   *   *   *   *

"How shall we divide our party for the motor ride, Ruth?" asked Harriet Hamlin about two o'clock on the afternoon of the same day.

Ruth's red car was standing in front of Mr. Hamlin's door with another larger one belonging to Harriet's friend, Charlie Meyers, waiting behind it.

The automobile party stood out on the side walk and Peter Dillon had somehow managed to be one of them.

"Suppose, Barbara, Grace and Hugh Post go along with me, Harriet?" Ruth proposed. "Mr. Meyers' car is larger than mine. He can take the rest of the party."

"What a division!" protested Peter Dillon, as he climbed into Ruth's automobile and took his seat next Bab. "Do you suppose, for one instant, that we are going to see Hugh Post drive off, the only man among three girls? Not if I can help it!"

The two automobiles traveled swiftly through Washington allowing the four "Automobile Girls" only tantalizing glimpses of the executive buildings which they passed on the way.

In about an hour the cars covered the sixteen miles that lay between the

Capital City and the home of its first President.

Such a deep and abiding tranquillity pervaded the atmosphere of Mt. Vernon that the noisy chatter of the young people was, for an instant, hushed into silence, as they drove through the great iron gates at the entrance to Mt. Vernon, and on up the elm-shaded lawn to the house.

Although it was December, the fall had been unusually warm and the trees were not yet bare of their autumn foliage; the grass still looked smooth and green under foot.

The "Automobile Girls" held their breath as their eyes rested on the most famous historic home in America.

"Oh, Ruth!" exclaimed Bab. But when she saw Peter's eyes smiling at her enthusiasm she stopped and would not say another word.

Of course, Mt. Vernon was an old story to Mrs. Wilson, to Harriet, and indeed to the entire party, except the four girls. But they wished to see every detail of the Washington house. They went into the wide hall and there beheld the key to the Bastile presented by Lafayette to General Washington. They examined the music room, with its queer, old-fashioned musical instruments; went up to Martha Washington's bedroom and even looked upon the white-canopied bed where George Washington died. Indeed, they wandered from garret to cellar in the old house. But it was a beautiful afternoon and the outdoors called them at last.

And, after all, it is the outdoors at Mt. Vernon that is most beautiful. The house is a simple country home with a wide, old-fashioned portico and gallery built of frame and painted to look like stone.

But there is no palace on the Rhine, no castle in Spain, that has a more beautiful natural situation than Mt. Vernon. It stands on a piece of gently swelling land that slopes gradually down to the Potomac, and commands a view of many miles of the broad and noble river.

Bab and Ruth managed to get away from the rest of their party and to slip out on the wide colonnaded veranda.

"How peaceful and beautiful it is out here," Ruth exclaimed, with her arm around her friend's waist. "It seems to me that, if I lived in Washington, I would just run out here whenever anything uncomfortable happened to me. I am sure, if I spent the day at Mt. Vernon, I should not feel trouble any more."

Barbara stood silent. A vague premonition of some possible trouble overtook her.

"Ruth," Bab asked suddenly, "do you like Harriet's friend, Peter Dillon? Every now and then he talks to me in the most mysterious fashion. I don't understand what he means."

Ruth looked unusually grave. Then she answered Bab in a very curious tone. "I know you have lots of common sense, Bab, dear," Ruth began. "But promise me you won't put any special faith in Peter Dillon. He is not one bit like Hugh, or Ralph Ewing, or the boys we met at the Major's house party. When I meet any one who is such a favorite with everyone I always wonder whether he has any real feelings or whether he is trying to accomplish some end. I suppose Peter Dillon can't help striving to be agreeable to everyone."

Bab laughed a little. "Why, Ruth," she protested, "that idea does not sound a bit like you. You are sweet to everyone yourself, dear, and everyone loves you. But I do know what you mean about Peter Dillon. I—"

"Hello," cried Mollie's sweet voice. She waved a long blue scarf toward Ruth and Bab. Mollie and Elmer Wilson were standing on the lawn, examining the motto on the sun dial. It read, "I record none but sunny hours."

"Let me write down that motto for you, Miss Thurston," Elmer Wilson suggested. "I hope you may follow the old sun dial's example and record none but sunny hours yourself."

"Ruth!" called Hugh, coming around from the other side of the porch with Peter Dillon. "Well, here you are, at last! It is not fair for you two girls to run off together like this. Harriet has disappeared, and Mrs. Wilson is hiding somewhere. Do you remember, Ruth, you promised to go with me to see the old Washington deer park. It has just been restocked with deer. Won't you come, too, Bab?"

Barbara shook her head as Hugh and Ruth walked off together. Bab felt sure that Hugh would like to have a chance to talk with Ruth alone, for they had never ceased to be intimate friends since the early days at Newport.

Peter Dillon stood looking out at the river, whistling softly, "Kathleen Mavourneen." It was the song Barbara had first heard him whistle in the drawing-room of Mr. Hamlin's house. The young man said nothing, for a few moments, even when he and Bab were alone. But when Bab came over toward him, Peter smiled. He had his hat off and he had run his hands through his dark auburn hair.

"I say, Miss Thurston, why can't you make up your mind to like me?" he questioned. "Surely you don't suspect me of dark designs, do you? You American people are so strange. Just because I am half a Russian you think I have some sinister purpose in my mind. I am not an anarchist, and I don't want to go about trampling on the poor. I wish you could meet the Russian ambassador. He is about the most splendid-looking man you ever saw. I know him, well, you see, because my mother was a distant cousin of his."

Barbara laughed good-humoredly. "You seem to be a kind of connecting link between three or four nations—Russia, America, China. What are your real duties at your legation?"

Barbara looked at her companion with a real question in her brown eyes—a question she truly desired to have answered. She was interested to know what duties an attaché performed for his embassy. Peter, in spite of his frivolities, claimed to be a hard worker.

"You have not seen the loveliest part of Mt. Vernon yet, Miss Thurston," Peter Dillon interposed just at this instant. "I want to show you the old garden, and we must hurry before the gates are closed. Yes; I know I did not answer your question. An attaché just makes himself generally useful to his chief. But if you really want to know what my ambition is, and how I work to achieve it, why some day I will tell you." Peter looked at Bab so seriously that she answered quickly:

"Yes, I should dearly love to see the garden."

Bab and Peter Dillon wandered together through the paths formed by the box hedges planted in Martha Washington's garden more than a century ago.

Neither seemed to feel like talking. The young man had seen the gardener as they entered the enclosure, and had persuaded him to allow them to go through the lovely spot alone.

Bab's vivid imagination brought to life the old colonial ladies who had once wandered in this famous garden. She saw their white wigs, their powder and patches and full skirts. So Bab forgot all about her companion.

Suddenly she heard Peter give a slight exclamation. They had both come to the end of the garden walk. There before them stood a great rose tree. Blooming in the unusually warm sunshine were two rose-buds, gently tipped with frost.

"Ah, Miss Thurston, how glad I am we found the garden first!" Peter cried. "This is the famous Mary Washington rose, which Washington planted here in his garden, and named in honor of his mother. Wait here until I find the gardener. I am going to make him let us have these two tiny rose-buds."

"How nice Peter Dillon really is," Bab thought. "Ruth was mistaken in warning me against him. Of course, he does not show on the surface what he actually feels. But perhaps I shall find out he is a finer fellow than we think he is. Mr. Hamlin says Harriet is wrong in believing Peter is never in earnest about anything."

"It's all right, Miss Thurston," called Peter, returning in a few minutes with his eyes shining. "The gardener says we may have the roses." The young fellow dropped down on his knees before the rose bush without a bit of affectation or self-consciousness. He skilfully cut the two half faded rose-buds from the stalk and handed one to Barbara.

"Keep this, Miss Thurston," he said earnestly. "And if ever you should wish me to do you a favor, just send the flower to me and I shall perform whatever task you set me to do to the best of my skill." Peter looked at his own rose. "May I keep my rose-bud for the same purpose?" he begged quietly. "Perhaps I shall send my flower to you some day and ask you to do me a service. Will you do it for me?"

"Yes, Mr. Dillon, I will do you any favor that I can," Bab returned steadily. "But I don't make rash promises in the dark. And I have very little opportunity to do people favors. You make me think of the newspaper girl, Marjorie Moore. She tried to force me into a promise without letting me know what she wanted, the first day I saw her. Does everyone try to get some one to do something for him in Washington?"

At the mention of Marjorie Moore's name the change in Peter Dillon's face was so startling that Barbara was startled. Just now he did not look in the least like an Irishman. His lips tightened into a fine, cruel line, his eyes grew almost black and had a queer, Chinese slant to them. It suddenly dawned on Barbara, that Russians have Asiatic blood in their veins and are often more like Oriental people than they are like those of the western world.

But Peter only said carelessly, after he had regained control of his face: "Miss Moore doesn't like me; and frankly, I don't like her. She told you she did society work for her newspaper. She does a great deal more. She is constantly watching at the legations to see if she can spy on any of their secret information. It is not good form to warn one girl against another. But if I were you, Miss Thurston, I would take with a grain of salt any information that Miss Moore might give you."

Barbara answered quietly: "Oh, I don't suppose Miss Moore will tell me any of her secrets. She does not come to Mr. Hamlin's except on business. Harriet does not like her."

"Good for Harriet!" Peter muttered to himself. "It may be Harriet, after all!"

"Barbara Thurston, you and Peter come along this minute," Harriet ordered unexpectedly. "Don't you know we shall be locked up in Mt. Vernon if we stay here much longer. Ruth's automobile is already filled and she is waiting to start. You and Peter are to get into Mr. Meyers' car with me. We have another hour before sunset. We are going to motor along the river and have our supper at an inn a few miles from here."

As Peter Dillon ran ahead to join Harriet Hamlin, a small piece of paper fell out of his pocket. Barbara picked it up and slipped it inside her coat, intending to hand it back to Mr. Dillon as soon as she had an opportunity. But there were other things that seemed of more importance to absorb her attention for the rest of the evening. And Barbara was not to remember the paper until some time later.

CHAPTER VI

After eating supper, and spending the evening at an old-fashioned Southern Inn on the Virginia side of the Potomac River, the two automobile parties started back to Washington.

Barbara and Peter Dillon occupied seats in the car with Harriet and Mr. Meyers, Mrs. Wilson, and two Washington girls who had been members of their party.

As Ruth did not know the roads it was decided that she keep to the rear and follow the car in front of her.

It was a clear moonlight night, and, though the roads were not good, no member of the party dreamed of trouble.

Bab sat next to Charlie Meyers, and her host was in a decidedly sulky temper. For Harriet had grown tired of his devotion, after several hours of it during the afternoon, and was amusing herself with Peter.

No sooner had the two cars sped away from the peaceful shadows of Mt. Vernon, than Peter began to play Prince Charming to Harriet.

Charlie Meyers did not know what to do. He was a stupid fellow, who expected his money to carry him through everything. He would hardly listen to Barbara's conversation or take the slightest interest in anything she tried to say.

Every time Harriet's gay laugh rang out from the next seat Charlie Meyers would drive his car faster than ever, until it fairly bounded over the rough places in the road.

Several times Mrs. Wilson remonstrated with him. "You are going too fast, Mr. Meyers. It is dark, and I am afraid we shall have an accident if you are not more careful. Please go slower."

For an instant, Mr. Meyers would obey Mrs. Wilson's request to lessen the speed of his car. Then he would dash ahead as though the very furies were after him.

As for Ruth, she had to follow the automobile in front in order to find her way, so it was necessary for her to run her car at the same high speed. Neither Ruth nor her companions knew the pitfalls along the road. Hugh did not keep his automobile in Washington, and, though he had a general idea of the direction they should take, he had never driven along the particular course selected by Mr. Meyers for their return trip.

Ruth felt her face flush with temper as her car shook and plunged along the road. In order to keep within a reasonable distance of the heavier car, she had to put on full power and forge blindly ahead.

Once or twice Ruth called out: "Won't you go a little slower in front, please? I can't find my way along this road at such a swift pace."

But Ruth's voice floated back on the winds and the leading car paid no heed to her.

Then Elmer and Hugh took up the refrain, shouting with all their lung power. They merely wasted their breath. Charlie Meyers either did not hear them or pretended not to do so. He never once turned his head, or asked if those back of him were making a safe journey.

Barbara was furious. She fully realized Ruth's predicament, although she was not in her chum's car. "Please don't get out of sight of Ruth's car, Mr. Meyers," Bab urged her companion. But he paid not the slightest attention to her request.

Bab looked anxiously back over the road. Now and then she could see Mr. A. Bubble's lamps; more often Ruth's car was out of sight. Patience was not Barbara's strong point.

"Harriet," she protested, "Won't you ask Mr. Meyers to slow down so that Ruth can follow him. He will not pay the least attention to me."

"What is your hurry, Charlie!" asked Harriet, in a most provoking tone. She knew the young fellow was not a gentleman, and that he was showing his anger against her by making them all uncomfortable. But Harriet was in a wicked humor herself, and she would not try to appease their cross host. She was having an extremely pleasant time with Peter Dillon, and really did not realize Ruth's difficulties.

The front car slowed imperceptibly, then hurried on again.

At about half past ten o'clock, Mr. Meyers turned into one of the narrow old-fashioned streets of the town of Alexandria, which is just south-west of Washington. The town was only dimly lighted and the roads made winding turns, so that it was impossible to see any great distance ahead.

Ruth had managed to keep her car going, though she had long since lost her sweet temper, and the others of her party were very angry.

"It serves us right," Hugh Post declared to Ruth. "We ought never to have accepted this fellow's invitation. I knew he wasn't a gentleman, and I know Mr. Hamlin does not wish Harriet to have anything to do with him. Yet, just because the fellow is enormously rich and gives automobile parties, here we have been spending the evening as his guests. Look here, Ruth, do you think I can forget I have enjoyed his hospitality, and punch his head for him when we get back to Washington, for leading you on a chase like this?"

Ruth smiled and shook her head. She was seldom nervous about her automobile after all her experiences as chauffeur. Yet this wild ride at night through towns of which she knew little or nothing, was not exactly her idea of sport.

Mr. Bubble was again outdistanced. As the streets were deserted, Ruth decided to make one more violent spurt in an effort to catch up with the front car. Poor Mr. A. Bubble who had traveled so far with his carload of happy girls was shaking from side to side. But Ruth did not think of danger. Alexandria is a sleepy old Southern town and nearly all its inhabitants were in bed.

"Aren't there any speed regulations in this part of the world, Hugh?" Ruth suddenly inquired.

But she was too late. At this instant everyone in her car heard a loud shout.

"Hold up there! Stop!" A figure on a bicycle darted out of a dark alley in hot pursuit of them.

"Go it, Ruth!" Hugh whispered. But Ruth shook her head.

"No," she answered. "We must face the music." Ruth put on her stop brake and her car slowed down.

"What do you mean," cried a wrathful voice, "tearing through a peaceful town like this, lickitty-split, as though there were no folks on earth but you. You just come along to the station with me! You'll find out, pretty quick, what twenty-five miles an hour means in this here town."

"Let me explain matters to you," Hugh protested. "It is all a mistake."

"I ain't never arrested anybody for speeding yet that they ain't told me it was just a mistake," fumed the policeman. "But you will git a chance to tell your story to the chief of police. You're just wasting good time talkin' to me. I ain't got a mite of patience with crazy automobilists."

"Don't take us all to the station house, officer!" Hugh pleaded. "Just take me along, and let the rest of the party go on back to Washington. It's awfully late. You surely wouldn't keep these young ladies."

"It's the lady that's a-runnin' the car, ain't it? She's the one that is under arrest," said the policeman obstinately.

Ruth had not spoken since her automobile was stopped.

She had a lump in her throat, caused partly by anger and partly by embarrassment and fright. Then, too, Ruth was wondering what her father would say. In the years she had been running her automobile, over all the thousands of miles she had traveled, Ruth had never before been stopped for breaking the speed laws. She had always promised Mr. Stuart to be careful. And one cannot have followed the fortunes of Ruth Stuart and her friends in their adventures without realizing Ruth's high and fine regard for her word. Yet here were Ruth and her friends about to be taken to jail for breaking the laws of the little Virginia city.

It was small wonder that Ruth found it difficult to speak.

"I will go with the policeman," she assented. "Perhaps he will let you take Mollie and Grace on home."

Of course no one paid the slightest attention to Ruth's ridiculous suggestion. Her friends were not very likely to leave her alone to argue her case before the justice of the peace.

"I say, man, do be reasonable," Hugh urged. He would not give up. "You can hold me in jail all night if you will just let the others go."

"Please don't argue with the policeman, Hugh," Ruth begged. "He is only doing his duty. I am so sorry, Mollie darling, for you and Grace. But I know you won't leave me."

"Oh, we don't mind," the two girls protested. "I suppose we can pay the fine and they will let us go at once."

Hugh said nothing, for he knew that he had only a few dollars in his pocket.

When Ruth's car finally reached the station house it was almost eleven o'clock.

The policeman took the automobile party inside the station. It was bitter cold in the room, for the winter chill had fallen with the close of the December day. The fire had died out in the air-tight iron stove in the room, and Mollie, Ruth and Grace could hardly keep from shivering.

"Well, where is the justice of the peace or whatever man we ought to see about this wretched business?" Hugh demanded.

At last the policeman looked a little apologetic. "I'll get some one to make up a fire for you," he answered. "I have got to go out and wake up the justice to look after your case. It's bed-time and he's home asleep."

"Do you expect us to sit here in this freezing dirty old room half the night while you go around looking up a magistrate?" Hugh demanded, wrathfully.

"I told you I would have the fire built up," the policeman answered sullenly. "But it ain't my fault you got into this trouble. You ought not to have broken the law. We have had about as much trouble with automobilists in this here town as we are willing to stand for. And I might as well tell you, right now, the court will make it pretty hot for you. It may be I can't get the justice to hear your case until to-morrow, and you'll have to stay here all night."

"Stay here all night!" cried the five young people, as they sank down into five hard wooden chairs in utter despair.

"Harriet, have you seen Ruth's automobile?" Bab asked, as Charlie Meyers' car got safely out of Alexandria and started on the road toward Washington.

Harriet and Peter both looked around and strained their eyes in the darkness. But there was no sign of Ruth or her party.

"Don't you think we had better go back a little, Charlie?" Harriet now suggested. "I am afraid you have gotten too far ahead of Ruth for her to follow you."

"What has Miss Stuart got Hugh Post and Elmer Wilson with her for, if they can't show her the way to town?" argued the impolite host of the automobile parties.

"I think Charlie is right, Harriet. I would not worry," interposed Mrs. Wilson, in her soft tones. "Elmer may not have known the road during the early part of our trip, but neither one of the boys is very apt to lose his way between Alexandria and Washington." Mrs. Wilson laughed at the very absurdity of the idea.

Harriet said nothing more, and, although Bab was by no means satisfied, she felt compelled to hold her peace.

"Will you leave me at my house, Charlie?" Mrs. Wilson demanded, as soon as their automobile reached Washington. "I know Harriet expects to make a Welsh rarebit for you at her home, but I am going to ask you to excuse me. I am a good deal older than you children, and I am tired."

When Barbara reached the Hamlin house she hoped ardently to see the familiar lights of her old friend, A. Bubble waiting outside the door. But the street was bare of automobiles.

There was nothing to do but to follow the other young people into the house and take off her hat and coat. But Bab had not the heart to join Harriet in the dining-room where the preparations for making the rarebit were now going on. She lingered forlornly in the hall. Every now and then she would peer anxiously out into the darkness. Still there was no sign of Ruth or any member of her party! Barbara was wretched. She was now convinced that some accident had befallen them.

"Come in, Barbara," called Harriet cheerfully. "The Welsh rarebit is done and it has to be eaten on the instant. I will make another for Ruth's crowd when they get in. They are certainly awfully slow in arriving."

"Harriet!" Barbara's white face appeared at the dining-room door. "I hate to be a nuisance, but I am dreadfully worried about the other girls. I know they would have gotten home by this time if nothing had happened to them."

Poor Barbara had to make a dreadful effort to swallow her pride, for Charlie Meyers had been dreadfully rude to her all afternoon. "Mr. Meyers," she pleaded, "won't you take me back in your car to look for my friends? I simply can't bear the suspense any longer." Barbara's eyes were full of tears.

"Oh, Bab, you are foolish to worry," Harriet protested. "It would not be worth while for you and Mr. Meyers to go back now. You would only pass Ruth on the road. It is nearly midnight."

"I know it is," Bab agreed. "And that is why I am so frightened. Don't you think you could take me to look for them? Please do, Mr. Meyers."

The ill-bred fellow shrugged his shoulders. "What do you take me for, Miss Thurston? I am not going to let my rarebit get cold. There is nothing the matter with your friends. They are likely to be along at any minute."

Barbara did not know what to do. Mr. Hamlin had not yet come in. Yet she must find out what had happened to Ruth, Mollie and Grace. Bab once thought of starting out alone and on foot, back up the long country road, but she gave up the idea as sheer foolishness.

At that moment the grandfather's clock in the hall chimed midnight.

Almost two hours had passed since the two automobiles had entered

Alexandria, and the little town was only eight miles from Washington.

Bab felt she was going to cry before Harriet's guests. She slipped her hand in her pocket to find her handkerchief. As she silently pressed her handkerchief against her trembling lips she smelt a delicate perfume. Something fresh and cool and aromatic touched her face. It was the tiny rose-bud Peter Dillon had presented to her in the garden!

Now Bab had determined never to ask Peter to do her a favor. She felt that, once she returned his pledge to him, he had the same right to ask a favor of her. But what could Barbara do? Her beloved sister and friends had certainly come to grief somewhere. And Bab was helpless to find them alone.

"Mr. Dillon," Bab spoke under her breath, just showing her handkerchief to him with the rose-bud crushed between its damp folds, "won't you help me to find Ruth?" Bab only glanced at the flower with a shy smile. But Peter saw it.

He jumped to his feet, his face flushing.

"Put the flower back, Miss Thurston," he said quietly to Barbara. "You do not need to ask me to help you look for your friends as a favor to you. I am ashamed of myself to have waited until you asked me. Harriet, I am going back to look for your guests."

Harriet, who was also feeling uneasy without being willing to confess it, cheerfully agreed.

"I am going to take your car, Meyers," declared Peter Dillon without saying so much as by your leave.

Bab and Peter Dillon hurried out to the waiting automobile. Both stopped only to take coats and caps from the rack in the hall.

If Peter Dillon wished to make a friend of Barbara Thurston, his prompt response to her plea for help came nearer accomplishing it than anything else in the world. When Peter refused Bab's proffered rose-bud she then determined to do him any favor that she could whenever he might desire to ask it of her.

CHAPTER VII

The next morning the "Automobile Girls" were sitting in the library of Mr. Hamlin's home. Ruth, Mollie and Grace were there, for Peter and Bab had secured their release from the Alexandria jail.

"But how do you think he ever accomplished it?" Mollie inquired.

Harriet laughed and flushed. "Oh, Peter accomplished it in the same way he does everything else—by making friends with people," she declared. "Girls, I hope you realize how ashamed I am of last night's proceedings. I never dreamed that anything had happened to you, or I should have certainly forced Charlie Meyers to turn back. But I think I have learned a lesson. Charlie Meyers was horribly rude to you, Bab, and I told him what we thought of him after you left. I don't want to see him again. So Father, at least, will be glad. Though how I am to get on in this world without a husband with money, I don't know." And Harriet sighed.

"Still I would like to have my questions answered," Mollie repeated. "How did Peter Dillon get us away from that wretched jail in such a short time when we thought we might have to stay there all night?"

"Why, he just found the justice of the peace, arranged about Ruth's fine, mentioned Mr. Hamlin's name and did a few more things," Bab laughed. "So, at last, you were permitted to come home."

"Poor Hugh and Elmer were so mortified at not having enough money with them to pay the fine. It was just an accident. Yet it was truly my fault," Ruth argued. "Father has always insisted that I take my pocket-book whenever I go out of the house. But, of course, I forgot it yesterday."

"Will Uncle Robert be very angry with you, Ruth, for being arrested?" Harriet asked. "He need never find out anything about it. Your fine wasn't so very large, and you always have money enough to pay for anything."

Ruth laughed. "Oh, I always tell Father every thing! I don't think he will be very angry with me, when he hears how we happened to get into trouble."

"Do you really tell your father everything?" Harriet asked, in a surprised tone.

"Why, yes; why not?" Ruth questioned.

Harriet shook her head. "Well, I do not tell my father all my affairs.

Oh, dear me, no!"

"I suppose I shall have to go back to Alexandria to-day, and appear at court," Ruth lamented. "I just dread it."

"Oh, no you won't," Bab explained. "Mr. Dillon said he would talk matters over with Mr. Hamlin, and that he had some influential friends over there. You will have to pay your fine, Ruth, but you probably will not have to appear at the trial. They will settle it privately."

"Girls," exclaimed Harriet, "I forgot to tell you something. There is a big reception at the White House to-morrow evening, and Father says he wishes to take the 'Automobile Girls' to present them to the President."

"How exciting!" exclaimed Grace Carter. "To think that the 'Automobile Girls' are going to meet the President, and yet you speak of it as calmly, Harriet Hamlin, as though it were an everyday affair."

"Oh, nonsense, Grace," Harriet begged. "It will be fun to go to the White House with you. You girls are so interested in everything. But a White House reception is an old story to me, and I am afraid there will be a frightful crowd. But which one of you will go shopping with me this morning?"

"I will," cried Mollie. "I'd dearly love to see the shops. We don't have any big stores in Kingsbridge."

"Is there anything I can get for you, girls?" Harriet asked.

Ruth called her cousin over in the corner. "Will you please order flowers for us to-morrow night!" Ruth requested. "Father told me to be sure to get flowers whenever we wanted them."

"Lucky Ruth!" sighed Harriet. "I wish I had such a rich and generous father as you have!"

"What can we wear to the President's reception to-morrow, Bab?" Mollie whispered in her sister's ear, while Harriet and Ruth were having their conference.

Bab thought for a moment. "You can wear the corn-colored frock you wore to dinner with the Princess Sophia at Palm Beach. It is awfully pretty, and you have never worn it since."

"That old thing!" cried Mollie, pouting.

"Suppose you get some pale yellow ribbons, Mollie, and I will make you a new sash and a bow for your hair," Bab suggested.

Pretty Mollie frowned. "All right," she agreed.

Harriet and Mollie did not go at once to the shops. They drove first to Harriet's dressmaker, the most fashionable in Washington.

"I must try on a little frock," Harriet explained. "We can do our shopping afterwards. I want you to see a beautiful coat I am having made, from a Chinese crepe shawl the Chinese Minister's wife gave me."

Madame Louise, the head of the dressmaking establishment, came in to attend to Harriet. The new coat was in a wonderful shade of apricot, lined with satin and embroidered in nearly every color of silk.

"Oh, Harriet, how lovely!" Mollie exclaimed.

"Yes, isn't it?" Harriet agreed. "But I really ought not to have had this coat made up. It has cost almost as much as though I had bought it outright. And I don't need it. I hope you have not made my dress very expensive, Madame. I told you to get me up a simple frock."

"Ah, but Miss Hamlin, the simple frocks cost as much as the fancy ones," argued the dressmaker. "This little gown is made of the best satin and lace. But how charming is the effect."

Mollie echoed the dressmaker's verdict as she gazed at Harriet with admiring eyes. Harriet's gown was white satin. Her black hair and great dusky eyes looked darker from the contrast and her skin even more startlingly fair.

Harriet could not help a little smile of vanity as she saw herself in the long mirror in the fitting room.

"Be sure to send these things home by to-morrow, Madame Louise," she demanded. "Father and I are going to take our guests to one of the President's receptions and I want to wear this gown."

Mollie gave a little impatient sigh.

"What is the matter, Mollie?" inquired Harriet, seeing that her little friend looked tired and unhappy. "I am awfully sorry to have kept you waiting like this. It is a bore to watch other people try on their clothes. I will come with you directly."

"Oh, I am not tired watching you, Harriet," pretty Mollie answered truthfully. "I was only wishing I had such a beautiful frock to wear to the reception to-morrow."

Madame Louise clapped her hands. "Wait a minute, young ladies. I have something to show you. You must wait, for it is most beautiful." The dressmaker turned and whispered to one of her girl assistants. The girl went out and came back in a few minutes with another frock over her arm.

Mollie gave a deep sigh of admiration.

"How exquisite!" Harriet exclaimed. "Whose dress is that, Madame? It looks like clouds or sea foam, or anything else that is delicately beautiful."

Madame shook out a delicate pale blue silk, covered with an even lighter tint of blue chiffon, which shaded gently into white.

"This dress was an order, Miss Hamlin," Madame Louise explained. "I sent to Paris for it. Of course it was some time before it arrived in Washington. In the meanwhile a death occurred in the family of the young woman who had ordered the dress. She is now in mourning, and she left the dress with me to sell for her. She is willing to let it go at a great bargain. The little frock would just about fit your young friend. Would she not be beautiful in it, with her pale yellow hair and her blue eyes? Ah, the frock looks as though it had been created for her! Do you think she would allow me to try it on her?"

"Do slip the frock on, Mollie," Harriet urged. "It will not take much time. And I would dearly love to see you in such a gown. It is the sweetest thing I ever saw."

Mollie shook her head. "It is not worth while for me to put it on,

Harriet. Madame must understand that I cannot possibly buy it."

"But the frock is such a bargain, Mademoiselle," the dressmaker continued. "I will sell it to you for a mere song."

"But I haven't the song to pay for it, Madame," Mollie laughed. "Come on,

Harriet. We must be going."

"Of course you can't buy the dress, Mollie," Harriet interposed. "But Madame will not mind your just slipping into it. Try it on, just for my sake. I know you will look like a perfect dream."

Mollie could not refuse Harriet's request.

"Shut your eyes, Mollie, while Madame dresses you up," Harriet proposed.

Mollie shut her eyes tightly.

Madame Louise slipped on the gown. "It fits to perfection," she whispered to Harriet. Then the dressmaker, who was really an artist in her line, picked up Mollie's bunch of soft yellow curls and knotted them carelessly on top of Mollie's dainty head. She twisted a piece of the pale blue shaded chiffon into a bandeau around her gold hair.

"Now, look at yourself, Mademoiselle," she cried in triumph.

"Mollie, Mollie, you are the prettiest thing in the world!" Harriet exclaimed.

Mollie gave a little gasp of astonishment when she beheld herself in the mirror. Certainly she looked like Cinderella after the latter had been touched with the fairy wand. She stood regarding herself with wide open eyes of astonishment, and cheeks in which the rose flush deepened.

"The dress must belong to Mademoiselle! I could not have made such a fit if I had tried," repeated the dressmaker.

"How much is the dress worth, Madame?" Harriet queried.

"Worth? It is worth one hundred and fifty dollars! But I will give the little frock away for fifty," the dressmaker answered.

"Can't you possibly buy it, child?" Harriet pleaded with Mollie. "It is a perfectly wonderful bargain, and you are too lovely in it. I just can't bear to have you refuse it."

"I am sorry, Harriet," Mollie returned firmly. "But I have not the money.

Won't you please take the gown off me, Madame!"

"Your friend can take the frock from me now and pay me later. It does not matter," said the dressmaker. "She can write home for the money."

For one foolish moment Mollie did dream that she might write to her mother for the price of this darling blue frock. Mollie was sure she had never desired anything so keenly in her life. But in a moment Mollie came to her senses. Where would her mother get such a large sum of money to send her? It had been hard work for Mrs. Thurston to allow Barbara and Mollie the slight expenses of their trip to Washington. No; the pretty gown was impossible!

"Do unbutton the gown for me, please, Harriet," Mollie entreated. "I really can't buy it." Mollie felt deeply embarrassed, and was sorry she had allowed herself to be persuaded into trying on the gown.

"Mollie!" exclaimed Harriet suddenly. "Don't you have a monthly allowance?"

Mollie nodded her head. Silly Mollie hoped Harriet would not ask her just what her allowance was. For Mrs. Thurston could give her daughters only five dollars a month apiece for their pin money.

"Then I know just what to do," Harriet declared. "You must just buy this frock, Mollie dear. I expect to have a dividend from some stock I own, and when it comes in, I shall pay Madame for the dress, and you can pay me back as it suits you. Do please consent, Mollie. Just look at yourself in the glass once more and I know you can't resist my plan."

Mollie did take one more peep at herself in the mirror. But if she had only had more time to think, and Harriet and the dressmaker had not argued the point with her, she would never have fallen before her temptation.

"You are sure you won't mind how long I take to pay you back, Harriet?" Mollie inquired weakly.

"Sure!" Harriet answered.

"All right then; I will take it," Mollie agreed in a sudden rush of recklessness, feeling dreadfully excited. For little Mollie Thurston had never owned a gown in her life that had cost more than fifteen dollars, except the two or three frocks which had been given to her on different occasions.

"Madame, you will send Miss Thurston's gown with mine, so she can wear it to the White House reception," Harriet insisted.

"Certainly; I shall send the frocks this evening," the dressmaker agreed, suavely. "But are you sure you will be in? I want you to be at home when the frocks arrive."

Several other customers had entered Madame Louise's establishment.

Harriet Hamlin flushed at the dressmaker's question. But she replied carelessly: "Oh, yes; I shall be in all the afternoon. You can send them at any time you like."

Before Mollie and Harriet had gotten out into the street, Mollie clutched Harriet's arm in swift remorse. "Oh, Harriet, dear, I have done a perfectly awful thing! I must go back and tell Madame that I cannot take that gown. I don't see how I could have said I would take it. Why, it will take me ages to pay you so much money!" Mollie's eyes were big and frightened. Her lips were trembling.

"Sh-sh! You silly child!" Harriet protested. "Here comes Mrs. Wilson. You can't go to tell Madame Louise you have changed your mind before so many people. And what is the use of worrying over such a small debt? The dress was a wonderful bargain. You would be a goose not to buy it."

Now, because Harriet was older than Mollie, and Mollie thought her very beautiful and well trained in all the graces of society, foolish little Mollie allowed herself to be silenced, and so made endless trouble for herself and for the people who loved her.

"Don't tell Barbara about my buying the frock, Harriet," Mollie pleaded, as the two girls went up the steps of the Hamlin home, a short time before luncheon. "I would rather tell Bab about it myself, when I get a chance."

"Oh, I won't tell. You may count on me," promised Harriet, in sympathetic tones. "Will Bab be very cross!"

"Oh, not exactly that," Mollie hesitated. "But I am afraid she will be worried. I am glad we are at home. I want to lie down, I feel so tired."

Not long after Harriet and Mollie had started off on their shopping expedition, Bab came across from her room into Ruth's.

"Ruth, do you think I could telephone Mr. Dillon?" she asked. "I picked up a piece of paper that he dropped in the garden yesterday, and I forgot to return it to him."

"Give it to me, child. I told you yesterday that I did not wish you to grow to be an intimate friend of that man. But I am writing him a note to thank him for his kindness to us last night. I can just put your paper in my letter and explain matters to him."

Bab carelessly tossed the sheet of paper on Ruth's desk. It opened, and Ruth cried out in astonishment. "Oh, Bab, how queer! This note is written in Chinese characters. What do you suppose Peter Dillon is doing with a letter written in Chinese?"

"I don't know I am sure, Ruth," Bab demurred. "It is none of our business."

"Did you get the yellow ribbon, Mollie?" Barbara asked her sister, two hours later, when Mollie and Harriet came in from their shopping. "I have been fixing up your dress all morning. It is awfully pretty. Now I want to make the sash."

"I did not get any ribbons, Bab." Mollie answered peevishly. "I told you I would not wear that old yellow dress."

CHAPTER VIII

Mollie Thurston was not well the next day. She stayed in bed and explained that her head ached. And Harriet Hamlin behaved very strangely. She was shut up in the room with Mollie for a long time; when she came out Mollie's eyes were red, and Harriet looked white as a sheet. But neither of the girls would say what was the matter.

Just before the hour for starting to the White House reception, Mollie got out of bed and insisted on dressing.

"I am afraid you are not well enough to go out to-night, Mollie," Bab protested. "I hope you won't be too disappointed. Shall I stay at home with you?"

Mollie shook her head obstinately. "I am quite well now," she insisted. "Bab, would you mind leaving me alone while I dress? I do feel nervous, and I know Ruth and Grace won't care if you go into their room."

"All right, Mollie," Barbara agreed cheerfully, wondering what had come over her little sister. "Call me when you wish me to button your gown. I have put the yellow one out on the lounge, if you should decide to wear it."

When Mollie was left alone two large tears rolled down her cheeks. Once she started to crawl back into bed and to give up the reception altogether. But, after a while, she walked over to her closet and drew out a great box. With trembling fingers Mollie opened it and gazed in upon the exquisite blue frock that had already caused her so much embarrassment and regret.

Should she wear the frock that night? Mollie Thurston asked herself. And what would Bab say when she saw it? For Mollie had not yet mustered up the courage to make her confession. Well, come what might, Mollie decided to wear her new frock this one time. She had risked everything to own it, so she might as well have this poor pleasure.

When Mollie joined Mr. Hamlin and the other girls downstairs a long party cape completely concealed her gown.

Mr. Hamlin did not keep a private carriage; so, as long as Ruth's automobile was in Washington, he decided to take his party to the White House in Ruth's car.

The girls were ready early, for Mr. Hamlin explained to them that they would have to take their position in the line of carriages that slowly approached the White House door, and that sometimes this procession was nearly a mile in length.

"I suppose you girls won't mind the waiting as much as we older people do, because you always have so much to say to each other. And perhaps this is my best chance to learn to know you better. I have been so busy that I have seen little of you during your visit to Harriet."

But Mollie and Harriet were strangely silent, and Bab felt absolutely tongue-tied before Mr. Hamlin. Fortunately, Grace and Ruth sat on each side of him.

"Mr. Hamlin," Grace asked timidly, "would you mind telling me what are the duties of the Secretary of State? Washington is like a new, strange world to us. I have learned the titles of the different members of the President's Cabinet, but I have not the faintest idea what they do. Mollie and I looked over the cards of the guests who came to your reception. Some of the cards just read: 'The Speaker,' 'The Chief of Staff,' 'L'Ambassadeur de France,' without any personal names at all."

Mr. Hamlin seemed pleased. The stern, half-embarrassed expression, that he usually wore before the girls relaxed a little at Grace's eager questioning.

"I am glad, Miss Carter, to find you take an interest in Washington affairs," he answered. "It is most unusual in a young girl. I wish Harriet cared more about them, but she seems devoted only to society." Mr. Hamlin sighed under his breath. "Yes; it is the custom for the officials in Washington to put only the titles of their office on their visiting cards. You are sure you wish to know the duties of the Secretary of State? I don't want to bore you, my child."

Grace nodded her head eagerly.

"Well, let me see if I can make it plain to you. The Secretary of State has charge of all the correspondence between the foreign countries and their representatives in the United States," Mr. Hamlin continued. "Do you understand?"

"I think I do," Grace answered hesitatingly, while Bab leaned over from the next seat to see if she could understand what Mr. Hamlin was explaining.

"The Secretary of State also receives all kinds of information from the consuls and diplomatic officers, who represent the United States abroad," Mr. Hamlin went on. "Sometimes this information is very important and very secret. It might bring on serious trouble, perhaps start a war with another country, if some of these secrets were discovered. The Secretary of State has other duties; he keeps the Great Seal of the United States. But my chief business as Assistant Secretary is just to look after the important private correspondence with all the other countries."

"Father," exclaimed Harriet, "why are you boring the girls to death with so much information? They don't understand what you mean. I have been living in Washington for four years, and I have not half an idea of what your duties are. But thank goodness, we have arrived at the White House at last!"

Their motor car had finally drawn up before the entrance to the Executive Mansion at the extremity of the eastern wing. The house was a blaze of lights; the Marine Band was playing a national air.

Harriet, who was familiar with all the rules that govern the President's receptions, quickly marshaled her guests into the lobby, where they had to take off their coats and hats.

Bab was so overcome at the enormous number of people about her, that she did not see Mollie remove her cape.

Mollie slipped quietly into a corner, and was waiting by Harriet's side, when Harriet called the other girls to hurry up the broad stairs to the vestibule above, where the guests were forming in line to enter the reception room.

Barbara, Ruth and Grace gave little gasps of astonishment when they first beheld Mollie. If little Mollie Thurston's heart was heavy within her on this brilliant occasion, she held her pretty head very high. The worry and excitement had given her a slight fever; her cheeks were a deep carmine and her eyes glittered brightly.

"Why, Mollie! What a vision you are!" exclaimed Ruth and Grace together. "Where did you get that wonderful gown? You have been saving it to surprise us to-night, haven't you?"

But Bab did not say a single word. She only looked at Mollie, her face paling a little with surprise and curiosity. How had Mollie come by a gown that was more beautiful than anything Bab had ever seen her sister wear? Barbara knew Mollie had not had the gown when they left home together, for she had packed her sister's trunk for her. But this was not the time to ask questions. Bab's mind was divided between the wonder and delight she felt at the scene before her, and amazement at Mollie's secret. "I do hope," she thought, as she followed Mr. Hamlin up the steps, "that Mollie has not borrowed that gown of Harriet. But no; it fits her much too well. Some one must have given it to her as a present and she has kept the secret until to-night to surprise me."

The "Automobile Girls" stood behind Mr. Hamlin and Harriet in the great vestibule just outside the famous Blue Room of the White House, where the President and his wife were waiting to receive their guests. The line was moving forward so slowly that the girls had a chance to look about them. Never had any one of them beheld such a beautiful spectacle. Of course the "Automobile Girls" had been present at a number of receptions during their brief social careers, but for the first time to-night they saw men in other than ordinary evening dress. The diplomats from other countries wore their superb court costumes with the insignia of their rank. The American Army and Navy officers had on their bright full dress uniforms.

Bab thought the Russian Ambassador the most superb looking man she had ever seen, and Mollie blushed when Lieutenant Elmer Wilson bowed gallantly to her across the length of the hall.

When the girls first took up their positions in the line, they believed they would never grow weary of looking about them. But by and by, as they waited and the number of people ahead of them only slowly decreased, they grew tired.

A girl passed by Barbara and smiled. It was Marjorie Moore. She was not going to try to shake hands with the President. She had a note book and a pencil in her hand and was evidently bent on business. Barbara also caught a glimpse of Peter Dillon, but he did not come up to speak to them.

Mr. Hamlin's charges at last entered the Blue Room. The President and his receiving party stood by a pair of great windows hung with heavy silk portieres.

It was now almost time for the "Automobile Girls" to shake hands with the
President. They were overcome with nervousness.

Harriet was next to her father; Bab stood just behind Harriet, followed by Ruth, Grace and Mollie.

"You are just supposed to shake hands with the President, not to talk to him," Harriet whispered. "Then the President's wife is next and you may greet the other women in the receiving line as you pass along. The Vice-President's wife stands next to the President's wife and the ladies of the Cabinet just after her."

Bab watched Harriet very carefully. She was determined to make no false moves.

Finally, Barbara heard her name announced by the Master of Ceremonies. She felt her heart stop beating for a moment, and the color mount to her cheeks. The next moment her hand was clasped in that of the President of the United States.

Barbara said a little prayer of thankfulness when she had finished speaking to all the receiving ladies. She felt glad, indeed, when Mr. Hamlin drew her behind a thick blue silk cord, where the President's special guests were talking in groups together. Bab then watched Ruth, Grace and Mollie go through the same formality.

Now nobody had ever warned Mollie that it was not good form to speak to the President before he spoke to her. She thought it was polite to make some kind of a remark when she was introduced to him. So all the way up the line she had been wondering what she ought to say.

As the President took Mollie's little hand he bent over slightly. For a very small voice said, "I like Washington very much, Mr. President."

The President smiled. "I am glad you do," he answered.

A little later, Mr. Hamlin took the girls through all the state apartments of the White House. One of these rooms was less crowded than the others. Groups of Mr. Hamlin's friends were standing about laughing and talking together. Barbara was next Mr. Hamlin when she happened to glance toward a far corner of the room. There she saw her newspaper friend. The girl made a mysterious sign to Barbara to come over to her and to come alone. But Bab shook her head.

Still she felt the girl's eyes on her. Each time she turned, Marjorie Moore again made her strange signal. Once she pointed significantly toward a group of people. But Bab only saw the broad back of the little Chinese Minister and the stately form of the Russian Ambassador. The two men were talking to a number of Washington officials whose names Barbara did not even know. Of course, Marjorie Moore's peculiar actions could not refer to them. But to save her life Bab could not find any one else nearby.

Womanlike, Barbara's curiosity was aroused. What could the girl want with her? Evidently, her news was a secret, for Miss Moore did not come near Mr. Hamlin's party and Bab simply could not get away without offering some explanation to them.

Barbara was growing tired of the reception. She had been introduced to so many people that her brain was fairly spinning in an effort to remember their names. Again Bab looked across at Miss Moore. This time the newspaper girl pointed with her pencil through a small open door, near which she was standing. Her actions said as plainly as any words could speak: "Follow me when you have a chance. There is something I must tell you!" The next instant Marjorie Moore vanished through this door and was lost to sight.

A few minutes later Bab managed to slip over to that side of the room. She intended merely to peep out the open door to see whether Miss Moore were waiting for her in the hall. Bab carefully watched her opportunity. Mr. Hamlin and the girls were not looking. Now was her chance. She was just at the door, when some one intercepted her.

"Ah! Good evening, Miss Thurston," said a suave voice.

Barbara turned, blushing again to confront the Chinese Minister looking more magnificent than ever in his Imperial robes of state.

The young girl paused and greeted the official. Still the Chinese Minister regarded her gravely with his inscrutable Oriental eyes that seemed to look her through and through. He seemed always about to ask her some question.

Of course, Barbara was obliged to give up her effort to follow Marjorie Moore, though she was still devoured with curiosity to know what the girl had wished to say to her. The next ten minutes, wherever Bab went, she felt the Chinese Minister's gaze follow her.

It was not until Barbara Thurston discovered that the Oriental gentleman had himself withdrawn from the reception room that she mustered up a sufficient courage to try her venture the second time.

"Miss Moore, of course, is not expecting me now," Barbara thought. "But as I have a chance, I will see what has become of her."

Bab peeped cautiously out through the still open door. She saw only an empty corridor with a servant standing idly in the hall. Should she go forward? No; Barbara did not, of course, dare to wander through the White House halls alone. She was too likely to find herself in some place to which visitors were not admitted.

The servant who waited in the hall saw Barbara hesitate, then turn back. He leaned over and whispered mysteriously: "You are to come to the door at the west side, which opens on the lawn. The young woman left a message that she would wait for you there."

"But I don't know the west side," Bab faltered hesitatingly, feeling that she ought to turn back, yet anxious to go on.

"The young woman said it was most important for her to see you; I can show you the way to the west door," the man went on.

Barbara now quickly made up her mind. Marjorie Moore was only a girl like herself. If she needed her or if she wanted to confide in her, Bab meant to answer the summons.

Bab found the portico deserted. There was no one in sight.

Down on the lawn, some distance ahead, she thought she saw a figure moving. Barbara drew her chiffon scarf more closely over her shoulders and ran quickly out into the garden without thinking. It was, of course, Marjorie Moore ahead of her. But Bab had not gone far, when the figure disappeared, and she realized her own foolishness. She must get back into the White House in a hurry before any one found out what she had done.

It was exceedingly dark out on the lawn in contrast with the brilliant illumination of the house, and Barbara was running swiftly. She had begun to wonder what explanation she could make if Harriet or Mr. Hamlin asked where she had been. As usual, Barbara was repenting a rash impulse too late. She ran obliquely across the yard in order to return in a greater hurry. Between a clump of bushes set at some distance apart her feet struck against something soft and heavy and Bab pitched forward across the object.

CHAPTER IX

Then Barbara Thurston's heart turned sick with horror. She recognized, in the same instant, that she had fallen over a human body. In getting back on her own feet, Bab was obliged to touch the figure over which she had fallen. She shuddered with fright. It could not be possible that any one had been murdered in the grounds of the White House, while a great ball was being given on the inside. Had Marjorie Moore expected foul play and called on Bab to help her guard some one from harm?

Barbara did not know what to do—to go on with her search for the newspaper girl, or go back to the White House and raise an alarm.

Bab was standing up, but she dared not look at the figure at her feet. She was now more accustomed to the darkness and she did not know what one glance might reveal.

"What a coward I am!" Bab thought. Trembling, she put out her hand and touched the body. It was warm, but the figure had fallen forward on its face. As Bab's hand slipped along over the object that lay so still on the hard ground, an even greater horror seized her. Her hand had come in contact with a skirt. The figure was that of a woman!

Barbara dropped on her knees beside the figure. She gently turned the body over until it was face upward. One long stare at the face was enough. The woman who lay there was the young newspaper girl who had summoned Bab to follow her but a short time before. She still had on her shabby evening dress. The pad and pencil with which she took down her society items lay at her side. But Marjorie Moore's face was pale as death.

Bab's tears dropped down on the girl's face. "My dear Miss Moore, what has happened? Can't you hear me?" Bab faltered. "It is Barbara Thurston! I tried to come to help you, but I could not get here until now."

The figure lay apparently lifeless, but Bab knew now that the girl was still alive. Bab did not like to leave her, for what dreadful person might not stumble over the poor, unconscious girl? Yet how else could Bab get help?

At this moment Bab looked up and saw a number of lighted cigars in the garden near the White House. Evidently a group of men had come out on the lawn to smoke. As Bab ran forward she saw one of the men move away from the others. He was whistling softly, "Kathleen Mavourneen, the bright stars are shining."

"Oh, Mr. Dillon!" cried Bab. "Poor Miss Moore has been dreadfully hurt and is lying unconscious out here on the grass. Won't you please find Mr. Hamlin, or some one, to come to her aid?"

"Miss Moore!" exclaimed Peter Dillon in a shocked tone. "I wonder whom the girl could have been spying upon to have gotten herself into such trouble? But, Miss Thurston, you ought not to be out here. Come back with me to the reception rooms. I will get some one to look after Miss Moore at once. It is best to keep this affair as quiet as possible."

"I can't leave the poor girl alone," Bab demurred. "So please find Mr. Hamlin as soon as you can. I will ask two of these other men to take Miss

Moore up on a side porch, out of the way of the guests."

The rest of the group of men now came forward; their uniforms showed they were young Army and Navy officers. One of them was Lieutenant Elmer Wilson.

"What a dreadful thing!" he exclaimed, as he and another officer, under Bab's directions, picked up Marjorie Moore's limp form and carried it into the light. "Some one has struck Miss Moore over the temple with a stick. She has a nasty bruise just there. But she is only stunned. She will come to herself presently."

Mr. Hamlin now hurried out with Peter Dillon, followed by Ruth and Harriet.

"Find our automobile; have it brought as near as possible. We must put the poor girl into it," Mr. Hamlin declared authoritatively. "Mr. Dillon is right. This affair must be kept an entire secret. It is incredible! Above all things, the newspapers must not get hold of it. It would be a nine days' wonder! Mr. Dillon, will you go to Miss Moore's paper? Say you feel sure the President himself would not wish this story to be published. Then you can find out where Miss Moore's mother lives, and see that she is told. The girl is not seriously injured, but she must be seen by a physician."

"But you are not going to take Marjorie Moore to our house, Father,"

Harriet protested. "She is so—" Harriet checked herself just in time.

She realized it would not be well to express her feeling toward the injured girl before so large a group of listeners.

"I most certainly do intend to take Miss Moore to our house," interrupted Mr. Hamlin sternly. "Her father was an old friend of mine whom changes in politics made poor just before his death. His daughter is a brave girl. I have a great respect for her."

In the excitement of helping their wounded visitor to bed, Barbara forgot all about Mollie's wonderful gown, and the questions she intended asking her. Bab and Ruth undressed Marjorie Moore, and stayed with her until the doctor and a nurse arrived. Then Bab went quickly to her own room and undressed by a dim light, so as not to disturb her sister. Mollie's face was turned toward the wall and she seemed to be fast asleep. There was no sign of the blue gown about to reawaken Bab's curiosity. Barbara was too weary from the many impressions of the evening and the fright that succeeded them, and hurriedly undressing she crept quietly to bed and was soon fast asleep.

CHAPTER X

It was almost dawn when Barbara began to dream that she heard low, suppressed sobs. No; she must be wrong, she was not dreaming. The sounds were too real. The sobs were close beside her, and Bab felt Mollie's shoulders heaving in an effort to hold them back.

"Why, little sister," cried Bab in a frightened tone, putting out her hand and taking hold of Mollie, "what is the matter with you! Are you ill?"

"No," sobbed Mollie. "There is nothing the matter. Please go to sleep again, Bab, dear. I did not mean to wake you up."

"You would not cry, Mollie, if there was nothing the matter. Tell me at once what troubles you," pleaded Barbara, who was now wide awake. "If you are not ill, then something pretty serious is worrying you and you must tell me what it is."

Mollie only buried her head in her pillow and sobbed harder than ever.

"Tell me," Bab commanded.

"It's the blue gown!" whispered Mollie under her breath.

"The gown?" queried Barbara, suddenly recalling Mollie's wonderful costume at the President's reception. "Oh, yes. I have not had an opportunity to ask you where you got such a beautiful frock and how you happened not to tell me about it."

"I was ashamed," Mollie sobbed.

Barbara did not understand what Mollie meant, but she knew her sister would tell her everything now.

"I bought the frock," Mollie confessed after a moment's hesitation. "That is I did not exactly buy it, for I did not have the money to pay for it. But Harriet was to pay for it and I was to give her back the money when I could."

"How much did the gown cost, Mollie?" Bab inquired quietly, although her heart felt as heavy as lead.

"It cost fifty dollars!" Mollie returned in a tired, frightened voice.

"Oh, Mollie!" Bab exclaimed just at first. Then she repented. "Never mind, Molliekins; it can't be helped now. The dress is a beauty, and I suppose Harriet won't mind how long we take to pay her back. We must just save up and do some kind of work when we go home. I can coach some of the girls at school. So please don't cry your pretty eyes out. There is an old story about not crying over spilt milk, kitten. Go to sleep. Perhaps some one will have left us a fortune by morning."

Barbara felt more wretched about her sister's confession than she was willing to let Mollie know. She thought if Mollie could once get to sleep, she could then puzzle out some method by which they could meet this debt. For fifty dollars did look like an immense sum to the two poor Thurston girls.

"But, Bab dear, I have not told you the worst," Mollie added in tones of despair.

"Mollie, what do you mean?" poor Bab asked, really frightened this time.

"Harriet can't let me owe the money to her. Something perfectly awful has happened to Harriet, too. Promise me you will never tell, not even Ruth! Well, Harriet thought she could lend me the money. But, the day after we got home from the dressmaker's, that deceitful Madame Louise wrote poor Harriet the most awful note. She said that Harriet owed her such a dreadfully big bill, that she simply would not wait for her money any longer. She declared if Harriet did not pay her at once she would take her bill straight to Mr. Hamlin and demand the money. Now Harriet is almost frightened to death. She says her father will never forgive her, if he finds out how deeply in debt she is, and that he would not let her go out into society again this winter. Of course, Harriet went to see Madame Louise. She begged her for a little more time, and the dressmaker consented to let us have a week. But she says that at the end of that time she must have the money from me and from Harriet. Harriet is dreadfully distressed. She simply can't advance the money to me for, even if the dividend she expects comes in time, she will have to pay the money on her own account. Oh, Bab, what can we do? I just can't have Mr. Hamlin find out what I have done! He is so stern; he would just send me home in disgrace, and then what would Mother and Aunt Sallie and Mr. Stuart say? I shall just die of shame!"

"Mr. Hamlin must not know," Barbara answered, when she could find her breath. Somehow her own voice sounded unfamiliar, it was so hoarse and strained. Yet Bab knew she must save Mollie. How was she to do it?

"Do you think, Bab," Mollie asked, "that we could ask Ruth to lend us the money? I should be horribly ashamed to tell her what I have done. But Ruth is so sweet, and she could lend us the money without any trouble."

"I have thought of that, Mollie," Barbara answered. "But, oh, we could not ask Ruth for the money! It is because she has been so awfully good to us, that I can't ask her. She has already done so much for us and she would be so pleased to help us now that somehow I would rather do most anything than ask her. Don't you feel the same way, Mollie?"

"Yes, I do," Mollie agreed. "Only I just can't think what else we can do, Bab. I have worried and worried until I am nearly desperate. We have only one week in which to get hold of the money, Bab."

"Yes, I know. But go to sleep now, Mollie. You are too tired to try to think any more. I will find some way out of the difficulty. Don't worry any more about it now." Bab kissed her sister's burning cheeks, whereat Mollie could only throw her arms about Barbara and cry: "Oh, Bab, I am so sorry and so ashamed! I shall never forget this as long as I live."

Bab never closed her eyes again that night. A little while later she saw the gray dawn change into rose color, and the rose to the blue of the day-time sky. She heard several families of sparrows discussing their affairs while they made their morning toilets on the bare branches of the trees.

At last an idea came to Barbara. She could pawn her jewelry and so raise the money they needed. She had the old-fashioned corals her mother had given to her on her first trip to Newport. There was also the beautiful ruby, which had been Mr. Presby's gift to her from the rich stores of his buried treasure. And the Princess Sophia had made Bab a present of a beautiful gold star when they were at Palm Beach. Barbara's other jewelry was marked with her initials.

Now Bab had very little knowledge of the real value of her jewelry, and she had an equally dim notion of what a pawn shop was. But she did know that at pawn shops people were able to borrow money at a high rate of interest on their valuable possessions, and this seemed to be the only way out of their embarrassment.

But how was Barbara to locate a pawn shop in Washington? And how was she to find her way there, without being found out either by Mr. Hamlin or any one of the girls?

Bab was still puzzling over these difficulties when she went down to breakfast.

"Miss Moore says she would like to see you, Barbara," Harriet Hamlin explained, when Bab had forced down a cup of coffee and eaten a small piece of toast. "Miss Moore is much better this morning, and a carriage is to take her home in a few hours. I have just been up to inquire about her. Father," continued Harriet, turning to Mr. Hamlin, "Miss Moore wants me to thank you for your kindness in bringing her here, and to say she hopes to be able to repay you some day. Marjorie Moore seems to think you discovered her out on the White House lawn, Barbara. However did you do it? I suppose you were out there walking with Peter Dillon. But it is against the rules."

"Does Miss Moore happen to know how she was hurt, Daughter?" Mr. Hamlin queried. "Lieutenant Wilson declares the girl was struck a glancing blow on the head with the end of a loaded cane. And the doctor seemed to have the same idea last night."

"Miss Moore does not understand just what did happen to her," Harriet replied. "Or at least she won't tell me. She declares she was out in the grounds looking for some one, when she was knocked down from behind. She never saw who struck her. How perfectly ridiculous for her to be running about the White House park alone at night! I wonder the guards permitted it. What do you suppose she was doing?"

"Attending to her business, perhaps, Daughter," Mr. Hamlin returned dryly. "Miss Moore works exceedingly hard. It cannot always be pleasant for a refined young woman to do the work she is sometimes required to do. I hope you will be kind to her, Harriet, and help her when it is within your power."

But Harriet only shrugged her shoulders and looked obstinate. "I should think Miss Moore would find the society news for her paper inside the reception rooms, rather than outside in the dark. It looks to me as though she went out into the grounds either to meet some one, or to find out what some one else was doing."

None of the "Automobile Girls" or Mr. Hamlin made response to Harriet's unkind remark and they were all glad when breakfast was over and the discussion ended.

Barbara at once went upstairs to the room that had been allotted to their wounded guest the night before. She found Marjorie Moore dressed in a shabby serge suit, lying on the bed looking pale and weak. A refined, middle-aged woman, with a sad face, sat by her daughter holding her hand. She was Marjorie's mother. The two women were waiting for the carriage to take them home.

"I want to thank you, Miss Thurston," Marjorie Moore spoke weakly. "I believe it was you who found me. I ought not to have asked you to come out into the yard, but I did not dream there would be any danger to either one of us. I want you to believe that I did have a real reason for persuading you to join me, a reason that I thought important to your happiness, not to mine. But I cannot tell you what it was, now; perhaps because I may have made a mistake. I must have been struck by a tramp, who had managed to hide in the White House grounds. I have no other explanation of what happened to me. But—" Miss Moore stopped and hesitated. "I have an explanation of the reason I wanted to talk to you alone. Yet I cannot tell you what I mean to-day. I want to ask you to trust me if ever you need a friend in Washington."

Bab thought the only friend she was likely to need was some one who could lend her fifty dollars. And Marjorie Moore was too poor to do that. She would have liked to ask the newspaper girl where she could find a pawn shop, but was ashamed to make her strange request before that gentle, sad-eyed woman, Marjorie Moore's mother.

So Barbara only pressed the other girl's hand affectionately, and said she was glad to know she was better, and that she appreciated her friendship.

CHAPTER XI

All morning Barbara pondered on how she could find a pawn shop in Washington, without asking questions and without being discovered. Her cheeks burned with humiliation and disgust at the very name pawn shop! Still Mollie must never know how much she dreaded her errand, and her mother must be spared the knowledge of their debt at any cost.

About noon the Hamlin house was perfectly quiet. Grace and Ruth had gone out sight-seeing and Harriet and Mollie were both in their rooms. Mr. Hamlin was over at his office in the State Department.

Bab had taken a book and gone downstairs to the library, pretending she meant to read, but really only desiring to think. She was feeling almost desperate. A week seemed such a little time in which to raise fifty dollars. Bab wished to try the pawn shop venture at once, so that in case it failed her, she would have time to turn somewhere else to secure the sum of money she needed.

Barbara was idly turning over the pages of her book, staring straight ahead of her at nothing in particular, when she unexpectedly leaped to her feet. Her face flushed, but her lips took on a more determined curve.

When Barbara Thurston undertook to accomplish a thing she usually found a way. Only weak people are deterred by obstacles.

Bab had remembered that she had heard Mr. Hamlin say that he kept a Washington directory in his private study. She knew that by searching diligently through this book she could find the address of a pawn shop.

Now was the time, of all others, to accomplish her purpose. With Bab, to think, was to do.

Barbara knew that no one was expected to enter Mr. Hamlin's study. She did not dream, however, that she would be doing any harm just to slip quietly into it, find the directory and slip quickly out again, without touching a single other thing in the room.

As has already been explained, Mr. Hamlin's study was a small room adjoining the drawing-room, and separated from it by a pair of heavy curtains and folding doors, which were occasionally left open, when Mr. Hamlin was not in the house, so that the room could be aired and at the same time shut it off from public view.

Bab went straight through the hall and entered Mr. Hamlin's study through a small back door.

The room was dark, and Bab thought empty when she entered it. The inside blinds were closed, but there was sufficient light through the openings for Barbara to see her way about perfectly. She was bent upon business and went straight to her task without pausing to open the window, for she wished to take no liberties with Mr. Hamlin's apartment.

The four walls of the study were lined with books, reports from Congress; everything pertaining to the business of the government at Washington. Certainly finding that old-time needle in a haystack was an easy duty compared with locating the city directory in such a wilderness of books.

First on her hands and knees, then on tip-toe, Bab thoroughly searched through every shelf. No directory could be found.

"I can hardly see," Bab decided at last. "It will not do any harm for me to turn on an electric light."

Bab was so intent on her occupation that, even after she had turned on the light, which hung immediately over Mr. Hamlin's private desk, she still thought she was alone in the room.

Lying under a heap of magazines and pages of manuscript on Mr. Hamlin's desk, was a large book, which looked very much as though it might be the desired directory.

Still Bab wavered. She knew no one was ever allowed to lay a hand on Mr. Hamlin's desk. Even Harriet herself never dared to touch it. But what harm could it do Mr. Hamlin for Barbara to pick up the book she desired?

She would not disarrange a single paper.

Bab reached out, intending to secure what she wished. But immediately she felt her arm seized and held in a tight grip.

A low contralto voice said distinctly: "What do you mean by stealing in here to search among Mr. Hamlin's papers?" The vise-like hold on Bab's arm continued. The fingers were slender, but strong as steel, and the grip hurt Barbara so, she wanted to cry out from the pain.

"Answer me," the soft voice repeated. "What are you doing, prying among Mr. Hamlin's papers, when he is out of the house? You know he never allows any one to touch them."

[Illustration: Bab Felt Her Arm Seized In a Tight Grip.]

"I am not prying," cried Bab indignantly. "I only came in here to look for the city directory. I thought it might be on Mr. Hamlin's desk."

"A likely story," interrupted Bab's accuser scornfully. "If you wished the directory, why did you not ask Mr. Hamlin to lend it to you? You wanted something else! What was it? Tell me?" The hold on Barbara's arm tightened.

"Let go my arm, Mrs. Wilson," returned Barbara firmly. "I am telling you the truth. How absurd for you to think anything else! What could I wish in here? But I needed to look into the directory at once—for a—for a special purpose," Barbara finished lamely.

Then her eyes flashed indignantly. "I am a guest in Mr. Hamlin's house," she said, coldly. "How do you know, Mrs. Wilson, that I have not received his permission to enter this room? But you! Will you be good enough to explain to me why you were hiding behind the curtains in Mr. Hamlin's study when I came in? You, too, knew Mr. Hamlin was not at home. Besides, Harriet receives her guests in the drawing-room, not in here."

"I came to see Mr. Hamlin on private business," Mrs. Wilson replied haughtily. "He is an old and intimate friend of mine, so I took the liberty of coming in here to wait for his return. But seeing you enter, and suspecting you of mischief, I did conceal myself behind the curtains. I shall be very glad, however, to remain here with you until Mr. Hamlin returns from his office. I can readily explain my intrusion and you will have an equal opportunity to tell Mr. Hamlin what you were doing in here."

Now Barbara, who had slept very little the night before, and had worried dreadfully all morning, did a very foolish thing. She blushed crimson at Mrs. Wilson's request. She might very readily have agreed to stay, and could simply have explained later to Mr. Hamlin that she had come into his private room because she needed to see the directory. But would Mr. Hamlin have inquired of Barbara her reason for desiring the directory? This is, of course, what Barbara feared, and it caused her to behave most unwisely. She trembled and fixed on Mrs. Wilson two pleading brown eyes.

"Please do not ask me to wait here until Mr. Hamlin returns," she entreated. "And, if you don't mind, you will not mention to Mr. Hamlin that I came into his study without asking his permission. Truly I only wanted to look at the directory, and I will tell Harriet that I have been in here."

Mrs. Wilson eyed Bab, with evident suspicion. "Why are you so anxious to see the directory?" she inquired. "If you wish to know a particular address why do you not ask your friends, the Hamlins, about it?"

"That is something that I cannot explain to you, Mrs. Wilson," said Barbara, a look of fear leaping into her eyes that was not lost on her companion.

"Very well, if you cannot explain yourself, I shall lay the whole matter before Mr. Hamlin the instant he comes home," returned Mrs. Wilson cruelly. "It looks very suspicious, to say the least, when a guest takes advantage of his absence to prowl among his private papers."

Tears of humiliation sprang to Barbara's eyes. It was bad enough to have Mrs. Wilson doubt her integrity, but it would be infinitely worse if stern Mr. Hamlin were told of her visit to his study. Bab felt that he would be sure to believe that she was deliberately meddling with matters that did not concern her. She looked at Mrs. Wilson. The forbidding expression on her face left no doubt in Bab's mind that the older woman would carry out her threat. Suddenly it flashed across the young girl that perhaps if Mrs. Wilson really knew the truth she would agree to drop the affair without saying anything to Mr. Hamlin.

"Perhaps it will be better after all for me to tell you my reason for being here," Bab said with a gentle dignity that caused Mrs. Wilson's stern expression to soften. "What I am about to say, however, is in strictest confidence, as it involves another person besides myself. I shall expect you to respect my confidence, Mrs. Wilson," she added firmly.

Mrs. Wilson made a jesture of acquiescence. Then Barbara poured forth the story of Mollie's extravagance and her subsequent remorse over the difficulties into which her love of dress had plunged both of the Thurston girls. "It is just this way, Mrs. Wilson," Bab concluded. "We have very little money of our own and we simply can't ask Mother to pay this debt. I won't ask Ruth to lend it to us because we are too deeply indebted to her already. I have some jewelry that is valuable; a ring, a pin and several trinkets, and I intend to take them to a pawn shop and borrow enough money on them to free Mollie of this debt. Then we will save our allowance money and redeem the things. I have never been in a pawn shop and don't know anything about them, so I thought I would find the address of a pawn broker in the directory and go there this afternoon. That is why I wanted the directory and why I came into Mr. Hamlin's study. Now that I have told you, perhaps you will feel differently about saying anything to Mr. Hamlin. He is so stern and cold that he would never forgive me if he knew of all this, although I am doing nothing wrong. It is very humiliating to be placed in this position, but now that the mischief has been done we shall have to pay for the gown and set it all down under the head of bitter experience."

Mrs. Wilson regarded Barbara steadily while she was speaking. There was a look of admiration in the older woman's eyes when Barbara had finished. "You are a very brave girl, Miss Thurston, to take your sister's trouble on your own shoulders. I am very glad that you saw fit to tell me what you have. I hope you will forgive me for my seeming cruelty, but I simply cannot endure anything dishonorable or underhanded. To show you that I believe what you have told me, and to prove to you that your confidence in me is well founded, I propose to help you out of your difficulty."

"You?" queried Bab in surprise. "I—I don't understand."

"I will lend you the money to pay the modiste," exclaimed Mrs. Wilson. "Then you shall pay it back whenever it is convenient for you to do so, and no one will ever be the wiser. We need tell no one that we met here in the study this afternoon."

"But—I—can't," protested Barbara rather weakly. "It wouldn't be right.

It would be asking entirely too much of you and—"

Mrs. Wilson held up her hand authoritatively. "My dear little girl," she said quickly. "I insist on lending you this money. I am a mother, and if my son were in any little difficulty and needed help, I should like to feel that perhaps some one would be ready to do for him the little I am going to do for you. Come to my house this afternoon and I will have the money ready for you. Will you do this, Barbara?" she asked extending her hand to the young girl.

Barbara hesitated for a second, then she placed her hand in that of Mrs. Wilson's. "I will take the money," she said slowly, "and I thank you for your kindness. I hope I shall be able to do something for you in return to show my appreciation."

"Perhaps you may have the opportunity," replied Mrs. Wilson meaningly.

"Who knows. I think I won't wait any longer for Mr. Hamlin. Come to my

house at half past four o'clock this afternoon. I shall expect you.

Good-bye, my dear."

"Good-bye," replied Bab mechanically, as she accompanied Mrs. Wilson to the vestibule door. "I'll be there at half past four."

CHAPTER XII

After the older woman had departed, Bab remained in a brown study. Had she been wise in accepting Mrs. Wilson's offer? Would it have been better after all to ask Ruth for the loan of the money? Bab sighed heavily. She had been so happy and so interested in Washington, and now Mollie's ill-advised purchase had changed everything. For a moment Barbara felt a little resentment toward Mollie, then she shook off the feeling as unworthy. Mollie had experienced bitter remorse for her folly, and Bab knew that her little sister had learned a lesson she would never forget. As for the money, it should be paid back at the earliest opportunity.

Barbara turned and went slowly upstairs to prepare for luncheon. She found Mollie sitting by the window in their room. Her pretty mouth drooped at the corners and her eyes were red with weeping.

"Cheer up, Molliekins!" exclaimed Bab. "I've found a way out of the difficulty."

"Oh, Bab," said Mollie in a shamed voice. "Did you have to tell Ruth?"

"No, dear," responded Bab. "Ruth knows nothing about it. Bathe your face at once. It is almost time to go down to luncheon, and your eyes are awfully red. While you are fixing up I'll tell you about it."

"Oh, Bab!" Mollie said contritely when her sister had finished her account of what had happened in the study. "You're the best sister a girl ever had. I don't believe I'll ever be so silly about my clothes again. This has cured me. I'm so sorry."

"Of course you are, little Sister," soothed Bab. "Don't say another word. Here comes Ruth and Grace."

The two girls entered the room at that moment and a little later the four descended to luncheon.

"I am going to do some shopping this afternoon," announced Ruth. "Would you girls like to do the stores with me?"

"I'll go," replied Grace. "I want to buy a pair of white gloves and I need a number of small things."

"I have an engagement this afternoon," said Harriet enigmatically. "I must ask you to excuse me, Ruth."

"Certainly, Harriet," returned Ruth. "How about you and Mollie, Bab?"

"Mollie can go with you," answered Bab, coloring slightly. "But would you be disappointed if I do not go? I have something else that I am obliged to see to this afternoon."

"Of course, I'd love to have you with me, Bab, but you know your own business best."

Suspecting that Bab wished to spend the afternoon in going over her own and Mollie's rather limited wardrobe, Ruth made no attempt to persuade Bab to make one of the shopping party, and when a little later A. Bubble carried the three girls away, she went directly upstairs to prepare for her call on Mrs. Wilson. It was a beautiful afternoon, and Bab decided that she would walk to her destination. As she swung along through the crisp December air the feeling of depression that had clung to her ever since Mollie had made her tearful confession vanished, and Bab became almost cheerful. She would save every penny, she reflected hopefully, and when she and Mollie received their next month's pocket money, she would send that to Mrs. Wilson. It would take some time to pay back the fifty dollars, but Mrs. Wilson had assured her that she could return it at her own convenience. Bab felt that her vague distrust of this whole-souled, generous woman had been groundless, and in her impulsive, girlish fashion she was ready to do everything in her power to make amends for even doubting this fascinating stranger who had so nobly come to her rescue.

By following carefully the directions given her by Mrs. Wilson for finding her house, Bab arrived at her destination with very little confusion. She looked at her watch as she ascended the steps and saw that it was just half past four o'clock. "I'm on time at any rate," she murmured as she rang the bell.

"Is Mrs. Wilson here?" she inquired of the maid who answered the bell.

"Come this way, please," said the maid, and Bab followed her across the square hall and through a door hung with heavy portieres. She found herself in what appeared to be half library, half living room, and seemed especially designed for comfort. A bright fire burned in the open fire place at one side of the room, and before the fire stood a young man, who turned abruptly as Bab entered.

"How do you do, Miss Thurston," said Peter Dillon, coming forward and taking her hand.

"Why—I thought—" stammered Barbara, a look of keen disappointment leaping into her brown eyes, "that Mrs. Wilson—was—"

"To be here," finished Peter Dillon, smiling almost tantalizingly at her evident embarrassment. "So she was, but she received a telephone message half an hour ago and was obliged to go out for a little while. I happened to be here when the message came and she told me that she expected you to call at half past four o'clock and asked me if I would wait and receive you. She left a note for you in my care. Here it is."

Peter Dillon handed Bab an envelope addressed to "Miss Barbara Thurston," looking at her searchingly as he did so. Bab colored hotly under his almost impertinent scrutiny as she reached out her hand for the envelope. She had an uncomfortable feeling at that moment that perhaps Peter Dillon knew as much about the contents of the envelope as she did.

"Thank you, Mr. Dillon," she said in a low voice. "I think I won't wait for Mrs. Wilson. Please tell her that I thank her and that I'll write."

"Very well," replied the young man. "I will deliver your message." He held the heavy portieres back for Bab as she stepped into the hall and accompanied her to the vestibule door. "Good-bye, Miss Thurston," he said with a peculiar, meaning flash of his blue eyes that completed Bab's discomfiture. "I shall hope to see you in a day or two."

Bab hurried down the steps and into the street. The shadows were beginning to fall and in another hour it would be dark. When she reached the corner she looked about her in bewilderment, then with a little impatient exclamation she wheeled and retraced her steps. She had been going in the wrong direction. She had passed Mrs. Wilson's house, when a murmur of familiar voices caused her to start and look back at it in amazement. Stepping off the walk and behind the trunk of a great tree, Barbara stared from her place of concealment, hardly able to believe the evidence of her own eyes. Peter Dillon was standing just outside the vestibule door, his hat in his hand and just inside stood Mrs. Wilson. The two were deep in conversation and Bab heard the young man's musical laugh ring out as though something had greatly amused him. Filled with a sickening apprehension that she was the cause of his laughter, Bab stepped from behind the tree unobserved by the two on the step above and walked on down the street assailed by the disquieting suspicion that Mrs. Wilson had had a motive far from disinterested in lending her the fifty dollars. She glanced down at the envelope in her hand. She felt positive that it contained the money, and her woman's intuition told her that Peter Dillon's presence in the house had not been a matter of chance. She experienced a strong desire to run back to the house and return the envelope unopened, and at the same time ask Mrs. Wilson why Peter had untruthfully declared that she was not at home. Bab paused irresolutely. Then a vision of Mollie's tearful face rose before her, and squaring her shoulders, she marched along through the gathering twilight, determined to use the borrowed money to pay Mollie's debt and face the consequences whatever they might be.

When Bab reached home she found that Harriet had come in and gone to her room, while the other girls had not yet returned. Barbara was glad that no one had discovered her absence, and divesting herself of her hat and coat she hurried up to her room. Closing and locking the door, she sat down and tore open the envelope and with hands that trembled, drew out a folded paper. Inside the folded paper was a crisp fifty dollar bill. Mrs. Wilson had kept her word.

While she sat fingering the bill, she heard voices downstairs and a moment later Mollie tried the door, then knocked. Bab rose and unlocked the door for her sister.

"Did you get it, Bab?" asked Mollie eagerly, a deep flush rising to her face.

"Yes, Molliekins, here it is," answered Barbara quietly, holding up the money. "To-morrow you and I will go to Madame Louise and pay the bill."

"Oh, Bab," said Mollie, her lips quivering. "I'm so sorry. I've been so much trouble, but I'll save every cent of my pocket money and pay Mrs. Wilson as soon as I can. It was so good of her to lend us the money wasn't it?"

Barbara merely nodded. Her early gratitude toward Mrs. Wilson had vanished, in spite of her efforts to believe in Mrs. Wilson, her first feeling of distrust had returned. She thought gloomily, as she listened to Mollie's praise of Mrs. Wilson's generosity, that perhaps after all it would have been better to pay a visit to the pawn broker.

CHAPTER XIII

In the meantime Harriet Hamlin was equally as unhappy as Bab and Mollie. For, instead of owing Madame Louise a mere fifty dollars, she owed her almost five hundred and she dared not ask her father for the money to pay the bill. The dividend, with which she had tempted Mollie to make her ill-advised purchase, amounted to only twenty-five dollars. It had seemed a sufficient sum to Harriet to pay down on her friend's investment, but she knew the amount was not large enough to stay the wrath of her dressmaker, as far as her own account was concerned.

Now, Harriet had never intended to let her bill mount up to such a dreadful sum. She was horrified when she found out how large it really was. Yet month by month Harriet had been tempted to add to her stock of pretty clothes, without inquiring about prices, and she now found herself in this painful predicament.

Harriet, also, thought of every possible scheme by which she might raise the money she needed. On one thing she was determined. Her father should never learn of her indebtedness. She would take any desperate measure before this should happen; for Harriet stood very much in awe of her father, and knew that he had a special horror of debt.

Since Charlie Meyers had behaved so rudely to Barbara, on the night of their automobile ride to Mt. Vernon, Harriet had had nothing to do with him. But now, in her anxiety, she decided to appeal to him. She could think of no other plan. Charlie Meyers was immensely rich and a very old friend. Five hundred dollars could mean very little to him, and Harriet could, of course, pay him back later on. She fully intended to live within her allowance in the future and save her money until she had paid every dollar that she owed.

But how was Harriet to see Charlie Meyers? After all she had said about him to the "Automobile Girls," she was really ashamed to invite him to her house. So Harriet dispatched a note to the young man, making an appointment with him to meet her on a corner some distance from the house on the same afternoon that Bab made her uncomfortable visit to Mrs. Wilson.

Charlie Meyers was highly elated when he read Harriet Hamlin's note. He had known her since she was a little girl in short frocks and was very fond of her. He had been deeply hurt by her coldness to him since their automobile party, but he was such an ill-bred fellow that he simply had not understood how badly he had behaved. He did know that Mr. Hamlin disliked him and did not enjoy his attentions to his daughter; so he hated Mr. Hamlin in consequence.

When Harriet's note arrived, he interpreted it to mean that she was sorry she had treated him unkindly, and that she did care for him in spite of her father's opposition. So he drove down to the designated corner in his car, feeling very well pleased with himself.

Harriet, however, started out to meet the young man feeling ashamed of herself. She knew that she was behaving very indiscreetly, but she believed that Charlie Meyers would be ready to help her and that she could make him do anything she wished. She accepted his invitation to take a ride, but she put off the evil moment of voicing her request as long as possible, and as they glided along in Meyers' car, she made herself as agreeable to her escort as she knew how to be.

After they had driven some distance out from Washington in the direction of Arlington, the old home of General Robert E. Lee, Charlie Meyers said bluntly to Harriet:

"Now, Harriet, what's the matter? You said in your note that you wanted to see me about something important. What is it?"

Harriet stopped abruptly and looked rather timidly at Meyers. She had been trying in vain to lead up to the point of asking her favor, and here her companion had given her the very opportunity she required.

Yet Harriet hesitated, and the laughter died away on her lips. She knew she was doing a very wrong thing in asking this young man to lend her money. But Harriet had been spoiled by too much admiration and she had had no mother's influence in the four years of her life when she most needed it. She was determined not to ask her father's help, and she knew of no one else to whom she could appeal.

"I am not feeling very well, Charlie," Harriet answered queerly, turning a little pale and trying to summon her courage.

"You've been entertaining too much company!" Charlie Meyers exclaimed. "I don't think much of that set of 'Automobile Girls' you have staying with you. They are good-looking enough, but they are kind of standoffish and superior."

"No, indeed; I am not having too much company," Harriet returned indignantly, forgetting she must not let herself grow angry with her ill-bred friend. "I am perfectly devoted to every one of the 'Automobile Girls,' and Ruth Stuart is my first cousin."

Harriet and Charlie were both silent for a little while after this unfortunate beginning to their conversation, for Harriet did not know exactly how to go on.

"I am worried," she began again, after a slight pause in which she counted the trees along the road to see how fast their car was running. "I am worried because I am in a great deal of trouble."

"You haven't been getting engaged, have you, Harriet?" asked the young man anxiously. "If you want to break it off, just leave matters to me."

Harriet laughed in spite of herself. It seemed so perfectly absurd to her to be expected to leave a matter as important to her happiness as her engagement to a person like Charlie Meyers to settle.

Charlie Meyers was twenty-two years of age. He had refused to go to college and had never even finished high school. His father had died when he was a child, leaving him to the care of a stepmother who had little affection for him. At the age of twenty-one the boy came into control of his immense fortune. So it was not remarkable that Charlie Meyers, who had almost no education, no home influence and a vast sum of money at his disposal, thought himself of tremendous importance without making any effort to prove himself so.

"No, I am not engaged, Charlie," Harriet answered frankly. "But I do want you to do me a favor, and I wonder if you will do it?"

The young man flushed. His red face grew redder still. What was Harriet going to ask him? He began to feel suspicious.

Now this rich young man had a peculiarity of which Harriet had not dreamed, or she would never have dared to ask him for a loan. He was very stingy, and he had an abnormal fear that people were going to try to make use of him.

Harriet had started with her request, so she went bravely on:

"I'll just tell you the whole story, Charlie," she declared, "so you will see what an awful predicament I am in. I know you won't tell Father, and you may be able to help me out. I owe Madame Louise, my dressmaker, five hundred dollars! She has threatened to bring suit against me at the end of a week unless I pay her what I owe before that time. Would you lend me the money, Charlie? I am awfully sorry to ask you. But I could pay you back in a little while."

Harriet's voice dropped almost to a whisper, she was so embarrassed. Her companion must have heard her, for he was sitting beside her in the automobile, but he made no answer.

Poor Harriet sat very still for a moment overcome with humiliation. She had trampled upon her pride and self-respect in making her request, and she had begun to realize more fully how very unwise she had been in asking such a favor of this young man. Yet it had really never dawned on the girl that Charlie Meyers could refuse her request. When he did not answer, she began to feel afraid. Harriet could not have spoken again for the world. Her usually haughty head was bent low, and her lids dropped over her eyes in which the tears of humiliation were beginning to gather.

"Look here, Harriet," protested the young man at last. "Five hundred dollars is a good deal of money even for me to lend. What arrangements do you want to make about paying it back?"

"Why, Charlie!" Harriet exclaimed. "You can have the interest on the money, if you like. I never thought of that."

"You can pay me back the interest if you wish," Charlie replied sullenly. "But you know, Harriet, that I like you an awful lot, and for a long time I've been wanting you to marry me. But you've always refused me. Now if you'll promise to marry me, I'll let you have the money. But if you won't, why you can't have it—that's all! I am not going to lend my good money to you, and then have you go your way and perhaps not have anything more to do with me for weeks. I tell you, Harriet, I like you an awful lot and you know it; but I am not going to be made a fool of, and you might as well find it out right now."

Harriet was so angry she simply could not speak for a few minutes. The enormity of her mistake swept over her. But silence was her best weapon, for Charlie Meyers began to feel ashamed. He was dimly aware that he had insulted Harriet, and he really did care for her as much as he was capable of caring for any one.

"I didn't mean to make you angry, Harriet," he apologized in a half frightened voice. "I don't see why you can't care for me anyhow. I've asked you to marry me over and over again. And I can just tell you, you won't have to worry over debts to dressmakers ever again, if you marry me. I've got an awful lot of money."

"I am very glad you have, Mr. Meyers," Harriet answered coldly, with a slight catch in her voice. "But I am certainly sorry I asked you to lend any of it to me. Will you never refer to this conversation again, and take me home as soon as you can? I don't think it is worth while for me even to refuse your offer. But please remember that my affection is something that mere money cannot buy." Harriet's tone was so scornful that the young man winced. He could think of nothing to reply, and turned his car around in shame-faced silence.

Harriet too was very quiet. She would have liked to tell her companion what she truly thought of him, how coarse and ill-bred he was, but she set her lips and remained silent. She did not wish to make an enemy of Charlie Meyers. After that day's experience, she would simply drop him from her list of acquaintances and have nothing more to do with him.

Stupid though he was, the discomfited young man felt Harriet's silent contempt. He wanted to apologize to her, to explain, to say a thousand things. But he was too dense to know just what he should say. It was better for him that he did wait to make his apology until a later day, when Harriet's anger had in a measure cooled and she was even more miserable and confused than she was at that time.

"I am awfully sorry, Harriet," Charlie Meyers stumbled over his words as he helped her out of his machine. "You know I didn't exactly mean to refuse your request. I'll be awfully glad to—"

But Harriet's curt good-bye checked his apologetic speech, and he turned and drove swiftly away.

CHAPTER XIV

"Mrs. Wilson's tea is at four o'clock, girls, remember," Harriet announced a day or so later, looking up from the note she was writing.
"Are you actually going sight-seeing again to-day before the reception? Truly, I never imagined such energy!"
"Oh, come, Harriet Hamlin, don't be sarcastic," Ruth rejoined. "If you had not lived so long in Washington you would be just as much interested in everything as the 'Automobile Girls' are. But Bab and I are the only ones to go sight-seeing to-day. Mollie isn't feeling well, and Grace is staying to console her. We shall be back in plenty of time. Why don't you lie down for a while! You look so tired."
"Oh, I am all right," Harriet answered gently. "Good-bye, children. Be good and remember you have promised not to be late."

Ruth and Bab were highly anxious for a walk and talk together, and they had a special enterprise on hand for this afternoon. Bab had received a mysterious summons from her newspaper friend, Marjorie Moore. The note had asked Bab to bring Ruth, and to come to the Visitors' Gallery in the Senate Chamber at an appointed time. Marjorie Moore chose this strange meeting place because she had a "special story" of the Senate to write for her paper and was obliged to be in the gallery.

Barbara was not particularly surprised at the request. She knew that Marjorie Moore had been wishing to make her a confidant ever since the reception at the White House. And she knew that the girl could not come to Mr. Hamlin's house because of Harriet's hostile attitude toward her.

So Bab confided the whole story to Ruth, and feeling much mystified and excited, the two girls set out for the Capitol.

During the long walk Barbara thought of her own secret, which she longed to confide to Ruth, but she dared not tell Ruth of the borrowed money for fear Ruth would at once insist on paying her debt. The money had to be paid, of course, and Bab hoped to pay it back at an early date, but she had not yet come to the point where she could bear to ask Ruth for it.

When Ruth and Bab finally reached the Capitol building, and made their way to the Visitors' Gallery in the Senate Chamber, Marjorie Moore was not there. She had failed to keep her appointment.

"I am not so very sorry Miss Moore has not come," Barbara remarked to Ruth. "She seems to be such a mysterious kind of person, always suggesting something and never really telling you what it is."

Ruth laughed. "The 'Automobile Girls' hate mysteries, don't they, Bab? But goodness knows, we are always being involved in them!"

The two visitors sat down to listen to the speeches of United States Senators. There was some excitement in the Chamber, Bab decided, but neither she nor Ruth could exactly understand what was going on. Both girls listened and watched the proceedings below them with such intensity that they forgot all about Marjorie Moore and her strange request.

A few moments later she dropped down into the vacant seat next to Barbara. She looked more hurried and agitated than ever. Her hat was on one side, and her coat collar was half doubled under. She was a little paler from her trying experience of a few nights before, and an ugly bruise showed over her temple. But she made no reference to her accident.

"I am sorry I am late," she whispered. "But come back here in the far corner of the gallery with me. I want to talk with you just half a minute. I am so busy I can't stay with you any longer. I just felt I must see you, Miss Thurston, before you go to tea with Mrs. Wilson this afternoon."

"Tea with Mrs. Wilson!" Bab ejaculated. "How did you know we were going to Mrs. Wilson's tea? And has that anything to do with your message to me?" Barbara did not speak in her usual friendly tones. She was getting decidedly cross. It seemed to her that she had been under some one's supervision ever since her arrival in Washington.

"Yes, it has, Miss Thurston," the newspaper girl replied quickly. "I want to ask you something. Promise me you will grant no one a favor, no matter who asks it of you to-day?"

Barbara flushed. "Why how absurd, Miss Moore. I really cannot make you any such promise. It is too foolish."

"Foolish or not, you must promise me," Marjorie Moore insisted. Then she turned earnestly to Ruth. "I know you have a great deal of influence with your friend. If she will not agree to what I ask her, won't you make her promise you this: She is not to consent to do a favor for any one this afternoon, no matter how simple the favor seems to be. Do you understand?"

Ruth looked at Marjorie Moore blankly, but something in the newspaper girl's earnest expression arrested her attention.

"I don't see why you won't make Miss Moore the promise she begs of you, Bab," Ruth argued. "It seems a simple thing she has asked you. And I don't think it is very nice of you, dear, to refuse her, even though her request does seem a little absurd to you."

"But won't you tell me why you ask me to be so exceedingly unaccommodating, Miss Moore?" Bab retorted.

Marjorie Moore shook her head. "That's just the trouble. Again I can't tell you why I ask this of you. But I want to assure you of one thing. It would mean a great deal more to me, personally, to have you agree to do the favor that may or may not be asked of you this afternoon. I am the only outside person in Washington who knows of a certain game that is to be played. It would mean a big scoop for my paper and a lot of money for me if I would just let things drift. But I like you too well to hold my tongue, though I am not going to tell you anything more. And I certainly won't beg you to do what I ask of you. Of course you may do just as you please. Good-bye; I am too busy to talk any more to-day." Before Barbara could make up her mind what to answer, the newspaper woman hurried away.

Ruth looked decidedly worried after Marjorie Moore's departure. But Barbara was still incredulous and a little bored at being kept so completely in the dark.

"Look here, Bab," Ruth advised, as the two girls walked slowly home together, "you did not promise Miss Moore to do what she asked of you. But you must promise me. Oh, I know it seems absurd! And I am not exactly blaming you for refusing to make that promise to Miss

Moore. But, Bab, we cannot always judge the importance of little things. So I, at least, shall be much happier at this particular tea if you will promise me not to do a single thing that any one asks you to do."

Both girls laughed gayly at Ruth's request.

"Won't I be an agreeable guest, Ruth?" Bab mimicked. "If any one asks me to sit down, I must say, 'No; I insist on standing up. Because I have promised my friend Miss Stuart not to do a single thing I am requested to do all afternoon.' I wish I did not have to go to Mrs. Wilson's tea to-day."

"You need not joke, Bab," Ruth persisted. "And you need not pretend you would have to behave so foolishly. I only ask you to promise me what you would not agree to, when Marjorie Moore asked it of you: 'Don't do any favor for any one, no matter who asks it of you this afternoon!'"

Bab gave up. "All right, Ruth, dear; I promise," she conceded. "You know very well that I can't refuse you anything, though I do think you and Miss Moore are asking me to be ridiculous. I do hereby solemnly swear to be, for the rest of this day, the most unaccommodating young person in the whole world. But beware, Ruth Stuart! The boomerang may return and strike you. Don't dare request me to do you a favor until after the bells chime midnight, when I shall be released from my present idiotic vow."

Mrs. Wilson's afternoon teas were not like any others in Washington. They were not crowded affairs, where no one had a chance to talk, but small companies of guests especially selected by Mrs. Wilson for their congeniality. So Mrs. Wilson was regarded as one of the most popular hostesses at the Capital and distinguished people came to her entertainments who could not be persuaded to go anywhere else.

Harriet and the four "Automobile Girls" were delighted to see a number of service uniforms when they entered the charming French drawing-room of their hostess, which was decorated in old rose draperies against ivory tinted walls.

Lieutenant Elmer Wilson's friends, young Army and Navy officers, were out in full force. They were among the most agreeable young men in Washington society. Lieutenant Elmer at once attached himself to Mollie; and his attentions might have turned the head of that young woman if she had not been feeling unusually sobered by her recent experience with debt.

Barbara soon recognized the two young men who had helped her carry Marjorie Moore from the lawn to the White House veranda. But neither one of them referred to the incident while there were other people surrounding them. Finally an opportunity came to one of the two men to speak to Barbara. He leaned over and whispered softly: "How is the young woman we rescued the other night? I almost thought she had been killed. We have been sworn to secrecy. But one of my friends has an idea that he saw the man who may have attacked Miss Moore. He was out on a porch before the rest of us joined him, and he swears he saw two figures at some distance across the lawn."

Bab shuddered. "I was on the lawn. Perhaps he saw me."

"No," her companion argued, unconvinced. "My friend is sure he saw two men; one of them was rather heavily built—"

Peter Dillon's approach cut short the conversation and the young Army officer turned away, as Peter joined Bab.

Barbara hardly turned around to greet the newcomer. She did not like Peter Dillon and she was very anxious to hear what her previous companion had to say. So Bab only gave Mr. Dillon her haughtiest bow. Peter did not appear discouraged; he stood for a moment smiling at Bab good humoredly, the boyish look shining in his near-sighted dark blue eyes.

Barbara was forced to speak to him. "How do you do, Mr. Dillon?" she asked at last.

"Very well indeed," replied the young man cheerfully. "Did you arrive home safely the other day?"

Barbara colored hotly. She felt certain now that despite her promise of secrecy Mrs. Wilson had betrayed her confidence and told Peter Dillon about the borrowed money. Why she had done so was a mystery and why he had lied to Bab in saying Mrs. Wilson was out was also a problem Bab could not solve.

While all this was passing through her mind Peter stood regarding her with a quizzical smile. Then he said smoothly: "Miss Thurston, will you do me a favor?"

Bab flashed a peculiar glance at him. "No," she replied abruptly.

The young man looked surprised. "I am sorry," he declared. "I was only going to ask you to go in the other room to look at a picture with me."

A little later in the afternoon, Harriet managed to get the four "Automobile Girls" together. "Mrs. Wilson wishes us to stay to dinner with her," Harriet explained. "She has asked eight or ten other people and Father has telephoned that he will come in after dinner to take us home."

CHAPTER XV

The dinner party was delightful. The "Automobile Girls" had not had such a good time since their arrival in Washington. Mrs. Wilson was a charming hostess. She was particularly gracious to Bab, and the young girl decided to forget the disquieting suspicions she had harbored against this fascinating woman and enjoy herself.

It was almost ten o'clock. Mr. Hamlin had not yet arrived at Mrs. Wilson's. Bab was sitting in one corner of the drawing-room talking gayly with a young Annapolis graduate, who was telling her all about his first cruise, when Elmer Wilson interrupted them.

"I am terribly sorry to break into your conversation like this, Miss Thurston," he apologized. "But Mother wishes to have a little talk with you in the library before you leave here. I am sure I don't know what she wishes to see you about; she told me to give you her message and ask no questions. May I show you the way to her!"

Bab's gay laughter died on her lips. She rose at once and signified her willingness to accompany Elmer to the library, but both young men noticed that her face had grown grave and she seemed almost embarrassed.

Elmer Wilson wondered why Miss Thurston had taken his mother's simple message so seriously. He was almost as embarrassed as Bab appeared to be.

When Barbara entered the room where she had received the envelope from Peter Dillon the room was but dimly lighted. Two rose-colored shades covered the low lamps, and great bunches of pink roses ornamented the mantel.

Mrs. Wilson wore a black and white chiffon gown over white silk and had a little band of black velvet about her throat from which hung a small diamond star. Her beautiful white hair looked like a silver crown on her head. She was leaning back in her chair with closed eyes when Bab entered the room, and she did not open them at once. She let the young girl stand and look at her, expecting her unusual beauty to influence Bab, as it had many other older people. Mrs. Wilson looked tired and in a softened mood. Her head rested against a pile of dark silken cushions. Her hands were folded, in her lap.

She opened her dark eyes finally and smiled at Barbara. "Come here,

Barbara," she commanded, pointing to a chair opposite her.

Bab looked at her beautiful hostess timidly, but her brown eyes were honest and clear. "You sent for me?" Bab queried, sitting down very stiff and straight among the soft cushions.

"Of course I did," Mrs. Wilson smiled. "And I should have done so before, only you and I have both been too busy. I am so glad you came to my tea to-day." Mrs. Wilson reached out her slender white hand and took hold of Barbara's firm brown one. "I want to make you a very humble apology," she continued. "I am very sorry that I was obliged to be away the other day when you called. I left the envelope with Mr. Dillon. I received your note yesterday, so I know that it was delivered into your hands. I did not return until after seven o'clock the other night, so it was just as well you didn't wait for me. I knew I could trust Mr. Dillon to give it to you."

The girl made no reply. She did not dare raise her eyes to the other woman's face for fear Mrs.

Wilson would divine from their expression that Bab knew she had lied. At the same time a thrill of consternation swept over her. What had been Mrs. Wilson's object in lending her the money? Bab was now sure that the loan had not been made disinterestedly. But what had Peter Dillon to do with it? It looked very much as though Mrs. Wilson and the attaché were playing a game, and were seeking to draw her into it. She resolved at that moment that she would write to her mother for the money, or ask Ruth for it. She would do anything rather than remain in Mrs. Wilson's debt. There was something about the intent way in which her hostess looked at her that aroused fresh suspicion in her mind. Bab braced herself to hear what she knew instinctively was to follow.

"I am so glad I was able to help you," Mrs. Wilson purred, continuing to watch the young girl intently. "I know that you meant what you said when you declared that you hoped to some day be able to do some favor for me. I did not think then that I should ever wish to take you at your word, but strange as it may seem, you are the very person I have been looking for to help me with a joke that I wish to play upon Mr. Hamlin. You know, Mr. Hamlin is a very methodical man. Well, I wagered him a dozen pairs of gloves, the other day, that he would misplace one of his beloved papers. And I hope to win the wager. What I wish you to do is to secure a certain paper from his desk and give it to me. He will never know how I obtained it. Of course I shall return it to him in a day or so, after he acknowledges his defeat and pays his wager."

Barbara shook her head. "I don't think I can take any part in any such joke, Mrs. Wilson," she said, looking appealingly at her hostess. "You don't really mean that you wish me to take one of Mr. Hamlin's papers without his knowledge, and then give the paper to you?"

"Certainly, child, I do mean just that thing," Mrs. Wilson said, laughing lightly. "You need not take my request so seriously. Mr. Hamlin will appreciate the joke more than any one else when I have explained it to him. Won't you keep your word and grant me this favor?"

"I can't do what you ask, Mrs. Wilson," Bab said slowly. "I'm awfully sorry, but it wouldn't be honorable."

Mrs. Wilson turned away her head, so that Barbara could not see the expression of her face. "Very well, Miss Thurston," she said sharply. "Don't trouble about it, if you think you will be committing one of the cardinal sins in doing me this favor. But don't you think you are rather ungrateful? You were perfectly willing to accept my offer the other day when you were in need of money to pay your sister's debt, but now you are in no hurry to cancel your obligation. I consider you an extremely disobliging young woman."

Barbara sat silent and ashamed. Yet she made no effort to propitiate her angry hostess.

The butler came to the library door to announce the arrival of Mr. Hamlin.

Barbara rose quickly. "I am so sorry not to be able to do you the favor you asked of me, Mrs. Wilson," she said in a low tone.

Mrs. Wilson did not reply. Then in a flash Barbara Thurston remembered something! It was the promise Marjorie Moore had asked of her, and which Ruth Stuart had insisted upon her making. Without recalling that promise at the time, Bab had still kept her word. She had been asked to do some one a favor—and she had refused. But of course Marjorie Moore must have had some other thing in mind when she made her curious demand. Now that Barbara thought again of her vow, she determined to be wary for the rest of the evening and to keep as far away from Peter Dillon as possible.

"I am going to play chaperon at your house in the near future, Harriet," Mrs. Wilson announced, as her guests were saying good night. "Your father says he is to be out of town on business and that I may look after you."

"We shall be delighted to have you, Mrs. Wilson," Harriet returned politely, though she wondered why her father had suddenly requested Mrs. Wilson to act as chaperon. Harriet had often stayed at home alone with only their faithful old servants to look after her, when her father went away for a short time. And now that she had the four "Automobile Girls" as her guests, she did not feel in need of a chaperon.

Peter Dillon had not spoken to Bab again during the evening, but had studiously avoided her, and Bab was exceedingly glad that he had kept his distance. But as she put on her coat to go home, she heard the rustle of a small piece of paper.

Barbara glanced down at it, of course, and found that some one had pinned a folded square of paper to the inner lining of her coat.

She blushed furiously, for fear one of the other guests would discover what had happened. Bab hated sentimentality and secrecy more than anything in the world. Inside the folded square of paper she found the tiny faded rose-bud, Peter Dillon had placed in his pocket that day when he had picked the two buds in the old Washington garden at Mt. Vernon.

On the way downstairs, Barbara still kept the flower in her hand. But when she found Peter's eyes were upon her she deliberately crushed the little rose-bud, then defiantly tossed it away.

CHAPTER XVI

It was the second day after Mrs. Wilson's dinner when Barbara made up her mind to tell Ruth of her debt to Mrs. Wilson and to ask her friend to lend her the money to relieve her of her obligation. Bab could endure the situation no longer. She simply determined to tell Ruth everything, except the part that poor Mollie had played in the original difficulty. She meant to explain to Ruth that she had needed fifty dollars, that she had intended going to a pawn shop to secure the money, her interview with Mrs. Wilson and her acceptance of the loan offered by the beautiful woman. She would not tell Ruth, however, why she had suddenly required this sum of money. Now, Bab knew Ruth would ask her no questions and would grant her request without a moment's hesitation or loss of faith. The sympathy between Ruth and Barbara was very deep and real.

It was one thing for Barbara Thurston to decide to appeal to Ruth's ever-ready generosity, but another thing actually to make her demand.

The two girls lay on Ruth's bed, resting. They had been to a dance at the British Embassy the night before. Mollie and Grace were together in the next room and Harriet was alone.

"Barbara!" exclaimed Ruth suddenly. "If you could have one wish, that would surely be granted, what would you wish?"

"I would like to have some money in a hurry," flashed through Bab's mind, but she was ashamed to make such a speech to Ruth, so she said rather soberly. "I have so many wishes its hard to single out one."

"Well what are some of them?" persisted Ruth. "Do you wish to be rich, or famous, or to write a great book or a play?"

"Oh, yes, I wish all those things, Ruth," Bab agreed. "But you were not thinking of such big things. What little private wish of your own did you have in your mind? Please don't wish for things that will take you far away from me," Bab entreated.

Ruth's blue eyes were misty when she replied: "Oh, no, Bab! I was just going to wish that something would happen so that you and I need never be separated again. I love you just as though you were my sister, and I am so lonely at home without you and Mollie. Yet, as soon as our visit to Harriet is over, you must go back to school in Kingsbridge and I have to go home to Chicago. Who knows when we shall see each other again? I don't suppose that our motor trips can go on happening forever."

Bab pressed Ruth's hand silently, her own thoughts flying toward the future, when she would perhaps be working her way through college, and teaching school later on, and Ruth would be in society, a beauty and a belle in her Western home.

"Why don't you say something, Bab?" queried Ruth, feeling slightly offended at Bab's silence. "Can't you say you wish the same thing that I do, and that you believe our motor trips will last forever?"

A knock at the door interrupted Bab's answer. When she went to open it a maid handed her three letters. Two of them were for Ruth and one for Barbara.

Ruth opened her letters quickly. The handwriting on one of them was her Aunt Sallie's. The other was from Ruth's father.

The postmark on Bab's letter was unfamiliar, however, so she did not trouble to open it, until she heard what Ruth had to say.

"Oh, I am so sorry!" Ruth ejaculated. "See here, Bab, Aunt Sallie writes us that she cannot come on to Washington. She has rheumatism, or something, in her shoulder and does not want to make the long trip. She says I had better come home in a week or ten days, and that Father will probably come for me. Of course, Aunt Sallie sends love and kisses all around to her 'Automobile Girls.' She ends by declaring I must bring you home with me."

Bab gave a deep sigh. "I do wish Miss Sallie had been here with us," she murmured.

Ruth looked reflective. "Have you any special reason for needing Aunt Sallie, Bab? I have an idea you have something on your mind. Won't I do for your confidant!"

"Yes, you will, Ruth!" Bab said slowly, turning her face to hide her painful embarrassment. "Ruth will you—"

Bab had picked up her own letter. More to gain time than for any other reason, she opened it idly. A piece of paper fluttered out on the bed, which Ruth picked up.

"Why, Bab!" she cried. "Look! Here is a check for fifty dollars! And there is some strange name on it that I never heard of before."

But Ruth could not speak again, for Bab had thrown her arms about her and was embracing her excitedly.

"Oh, Ruth, I am so glad, I am so glad!" Bab exclaimed, half laughing, half crying. "Just think of it—fifty dollars! And just now of all times. I never dreamed of such luck coming to me. It is just too wonderful!"

"Barbara Thurston, will you be quiet and tell me what has happened to you?" Ruth insisted. "You haven't lost your wits, have you, child?"

"No, I have found them," Bab declared. "More wits than I ever dreamed I had. Now, Ruth, don't be cross with me because I never confided this to you before. But I have not told a single person until to-day, not even Mother or Mollie. Months before I came to Washington, just before school commenced, I saw a notice in a newspaper, saying that a prize would be given for a short story written by a schoolgirl between the ages of sixteen and eighteen. So, up in the little attic at Laurel Cottage, I wrote a story. I worked on it for days and days, and then I sent it off to the publisher. I was ashamed to tell any one that I had written it, and never dreamed I should hear of it again. But now I have won the prize of fifty dollars,"

Bab stood up on the bed waving her check in one hand and, holding the skirt of her blue kimono in the other, executed a few jubilant dance steps.

"Oh, Barbara, I am so proud!" Ruth rejoined, looking fully as happy as Bab. "Just think how clever you are! The fame of being an author is more desirable than the money. I must tell Mollie and Grace all about it."

[Illustration: "Oh, Ruth, I Am So Glad!"]

But Mollie and Grace had been attracted by the excitement in the next room, and now rushed in to hear the news.

Mollie's eyes filled with tears as she embraced her sister. She knew how Bab's fifty dollars must be used, and why her sister was so delighted with her success.

"What are you going to do with the fifty dollars, Bab?" Grace inquired.

"I suppose you will put it away for your college money."

Bab did not reply. She was already longing for a little time to herself, a pen, and ink and note paper.

Harriet came in now with a message:

"Children," she said, "it is time to dress for dinner. I have just had a telephone call from Father. He is going out of town to-night, but Mrs. Wilson is to stay with us. Father is not going until after dinner, and Mrs. Wilson and Elmer and Peter Dillon will be here to dine with us. So we shall have rather a jolly party. You girls had better dress."

Harriet's was at once informed of Bab's good luck, and in offering Barbara her congratulations she forgot to tell the rest of her story.

Harriet had asked her father to come home half an hour before his guests arrived. She had almost persuaded herself to make a full confession of her fault. But the tangle of circumstance was not to be so easily unraveled.

Before Bab went down to dinner she slipped over to her desk and indorsed the check, put it in an envelope, and hid the envelope inside her dress. Her heart was lighter than it had been in weeks, for she believed her own and Mollie's share in the Washington trouble was over.

Mr. William Hamlin was late to dinner and his guests were compelled to hurry through the meal on his account, as he wished to catch a special train out of the city. But they had a gay dinner party nevertheless and Harriet did not know whether she was sorry or glad that her confession had been delayed.

After Mr. Hamlin had said good-bye to his visitors Harriet followed her father out into the hall. She thought if she told him of her fault just before he went away his anger would have time to cool before he could have opportunity to do more than reproach her for her extravagance.

"Father," Harriet whispered timidly, "can't you wait a few minutes longer? I told you there was something I had to tell you."

Mr. Hamlin shook his head impatiently. "No, Harriet, this is not the time nor the place for confidences. I am in far too much of a hurry. If you want to ask me for money I positively haven't any to give you. Now run on back to your guests."

Harriet turned slowly away, and so Mr. Hamlin lost his chance to set matters straight.

Just before he went out the door, he called back to his daughter:

"Oh, Harriet, I have left the key to my strong box on my study table. Don't forget to put it away for me; it is most important that you do so, for I really have not time to turn back."

During the entire evening Peter Dillon devoted himself exclusively to Harriet, and Bab was vastly relieved that he did not approach her. She decided that he fully understood that she did not consider the pledge of the faded rose-bud, binding. Mrs. Wilson had apparently forgotten Bab's refusal of her request. She was as cordial to Barbara as she was to Harriet, or to any of the

"Automobile Girls."

It was after midnight when Mrs. Wilson told Elmer and Peter that they must both go home. Bab's envelope was still tucked inside her dress. She had had no chance so far to give it to Mrs. Wilson. After Peter and Elmer had gone, however, and the girls trooped upstairs to bed, laughing and chatting gayly, Bab found a chance to slip the troublesome envelope into Mrs. Wilson's hand. With a whispered, "In the envelope is a check for the money I borrowed. I thank you so much for your kindness," Bab ran down the hall to her own room, feeling more at ease in her mind than she had since Mollie's confession.

As for Harriet, she was so fully occupied with her guests that her father's command to secure the key of his strong box, which he had left on his study table, slipped from her mind and she retired without giving the matter a second thought.

CHAPTER XVII

Long after every one had retired Ruth Stuart lay wide awake. Try as she might, sleep refused to visit her eyelids. At last, after she had counted innumerable sheep and was wider awake than ever, she resolved to go and waken Bab. Ruth moved about in the dark carefully, in order not to arouse Grace, with whom she roomed, found her dressing-gown and slippers, and tip-toed softly into Barbara's room. She knew that Barbara would not resent being awakened even at that unseasonable hour.

"Barbara, are you awake?" she whispered, coming up to Bab's bed and laying a gentle hand on her friend's face. "I want to talk with you and I am so thirsty. Won't you come downstairs with me to get a drink of water?"

Bab turned over sleepily and yawned: "Isn't there always some water in the hall, Ruth? I am so tired I can't wake up," she declared.

But Ruth gave her another shake. Barbara crawled slowly out of bed, while
Ruth found her bedroom slippers and wrapped her in her warm bathrobe.
Then both girls stole softly out into the dark hall.

At the head of the stairs there was a broad landing. On this landing, just under a stained glass window, there was a leather couch and a table, which always held a pitcher of drinking water. On the window ledge the servants were required to keep a candle, so that anyone who wished to do so might find his way downstairs at night, without difficulty.

The two girls made their way slowly to this spot, and Bab felt along the sill for the candle. It was not in its accustomed place.

"I can't find the candle, Ruth," Bab whispered. "But you know where to find the water. Just fumble until you get hold of the pitcher."

"Won't you have a glass of water?" Ruth invited, pushing the tumbler under Bab's very nose. Then the two girls began to giggle softly.

"No, thank you," Bab answered decidedly. "Come, thirsty maiden! Who took me from my nice warm bed? Ruth Stuart! Let's go back upstairs and get to sleep again in a hurry."

But for answer, Ruth drew Barbara down on the old leather couch in the complete darkness and put her arms about her.

"Don't go back to bed, Bab. I'm not a bit sleepy. That's why I dragged you out of bed. I couldn't go to sleep and I just had to have company. Be a nice Bab and let's sit here and exchange conversation."

"All right," Bab replied amiably, snuggling up closer to her friend.
"Dear me, isn't it cold and dark and quiet out here!"

Ruth gave a faint shiver. Then both girls sat absolutely still without speaking or moving—they had heard an unmistakable sound in the hall below them. The noise was so slight it could hardly be called a sound. Yet even this slight movement did not belong to the night and the silence of the sleeping household.

The sound was repeated. Then a stillness followed, more absolute than before.

"Is it a burglar, Bab?" Ruth breathed.

Barbara's hand pressure meant they must listen and wait. "It may be possible," Bab thought, "that a dog or cat has somehow gotten into the house downstairs."

At this, the girls left the sofa and, going over to the banister, peered cautiously down into the darkness.

This time the two girls saw a light that shone like a flame in the darkness below. Quietly there floated into their line of vision something white, ethereal—perchance a spirit from another world. It vanished and the blackness was again unbroken. The figure had seemed strangely tall. It appeared to swim along, rather than to walk, draperies as fine as mist hanging about it.

"What on earth was that, Barbara?" Ruth queried, more curious than frightened by the apparition. "If I believed in spirits I might think we had just seen the ghost of Harriet's mother. Harriet's old black Mammy has always said that Aunt Hattie comes back at night to guard Harriet, if she is in any special trouble or danger."

"I suppose we had better go downstairs and find out what we have seen," whispered more matter-of-fact Bab. "Mr. Hamlin is not here. I don't think there is any sense in our arousing the family until we know something more. I should not like to frighten Mrs. Wilson and Harriet for nothing."

The two girls slipped downstairs without making a sound. Everything on the lower floor seemed dark and quiet. Ruth and Bab both began to think they had been haunted by a dream. They were on their way upstairs again, when Ruth suddenly turned and glanced behind her.

"Bab," she whispered, clutching at Barbara's bathrobe until that young woman nearly tumbled backwards down the steps, "there is a light in Uncle's study! I suppose it is Harriet who is down there."

It flashed across Bab's mind to wonder, oddly, if Harriet's visit to her father's study at night could have anything to do with her debt to her dressmaker of five hundred dollars! For Mollie had reported to her sister that Harriet was feeling desperate over her unpleasant situation.

"If it is Harriet downstairs I don't think we ought to go down," Bab objected. "We would frighten her if we walked in on her so unexpectedly."

"Harriet ought not to be alone downstairs," Ruth insisted. "Uncle would not like it. I am going to peep in on her, and then make her come on upstairs to bed."

Ruth led the way, with Bab at her heels. But it occurred to Barbara that the midnight visitor to Mr. Hamlin's study might be some one other than his daughter. Bab did not know whether Mr. Hamlin kept any money in his strong box in the study. She and Ruth were both unarmed, and might be approaching an unknown danger. Quick as a flash Bab arranged a little scheme of defense.

There were two old-fashioned square stools placed on opposite sides of the hall. Without a word to Ruth, who was intent on her errand, Bab drew out these two stools and placed them side by side in the immediate centre of the hall. Any one who tried to escape from the study would stumble over these stools and at once alarm the household. Of course, if Bab and Ruth found Harriet in her father's study Bab could warn them of her trap.

"What shall we do, Bab?" Ruth asked when Barbara joined her. "The light is still shining in the study. But I do not want to knock on the door; it would frighten Harriet. And it would terrify her even more if we walked right into the study out of this darkness. But we can't wait out here all night. I am catching cold."

Barbara did not reply. They were in a difficult situation. Suppose Harriet were in the study? They did not wish to frighten her. In case the veiled figure was not Harriet any speech of theirs would give their presence away.

"I think we had better open the door quickly and rush in," Ruth now decided. "Then Harriet can see at once who we are."

Without waiting for further consultation with Bab, Ruth flung wide the study door.

In the same instant the light in the room went out like a flash.

"Harriet, is that you?" Ruth faltered. There was no answer, save some one's quick breathing. Ruth and Bab could both perceive that an absolutely white figure was crouched in a corner of the room in the dark.

Bab moved cautiously toward the spot where she knew an electric light swung just above Mr. Hamlin's desk. But it was so dark that she had to move her hand gropingly above her head, for a moment, in order to locate the light.

The veiled being in the corner must have guessed her motive. Like a zephyr it floated past the two girls. So light and swift was its movement that Bab's hand was arrested in its design. Surely a ghost, not a human creature, had passed by them.

The next sound that Ruth and Bab heard was not ghostlike. It was very human. First came a crash, then a cry of terror and surprise.

At the same moment Bab found the light she sought, turned it on, and Ruth rushed out into the hall.

There on the floor Ruth discovered a jumble of stools and white draperies. And, shaking with the shock of her fall and forced laughter, was—not Harriet, but her guest, Mrs. Wilson! She had a long white chiffon veil over her head, a filmy shawl over her shoulders, and a white gown. With her white hair she made a very satisfactory picture of a ghost.

"My dear Mrs. Wilson!" cried Ruth, in horrified tones, "What has happened to you? Were you walking in your sleep! Do let me help you up. I did not know these stools were out here where you could stumble over them."

Bab stood gravely looking on at the scene without expressing such marked surprise.

Mrs. Wilson gave one curious, malignant glance at Bab, then she smiled:

"Help me up, children. I am fairly caught in my crime."

Bab took hold of Mrs. Wilson by one arm, Ruth grasped her by the other, and they both struggled to lift her. Mrs. Wilson gave a slight groan as she got fairly on her feet. Her right hand clutched Bab for added support. In falling over the stools Mrs. Wilson had given her knee a severe wrench.

At the moment she staggered, Barbara saw a large, oblong envelope fall to the floor from under Mrs. Wilson's soft white draperies.

"What is the trouble?" called Harriet, Mollie and Grace, poking their three sleepy heads over the banisters.

At this interruption Bab stooped down and quickly caught up the envelope, while Mrs. Wilson's attention was distracted by the three girls who were rapidly descending the steps.

"Mrs. Wilson came downstairs for something," Ruth explained in her quiet, well-bred fashion. "Bab and I heard a noise and, as we did not recognize her, we followed her. We frightened Mrs. Wilson so that she stumbled over these stools out in the hall. I am afraid she is a little hurt. I think you had better call the servants, Harriet."

Ruth did not, for an instant, let the surprise she felt at Mrs. Wilson's extraordinary conduct appear in her voice.

"No, don't call any of the servants to-night, Harriet," Mrs. Wilson demurred. "I am all right now. I owe you children an apology for my conduct to-night and also an explanation. But I think I can explain everything much more satisfactorily if we wait until morning. I think Miss Thurston already understands my escapade. I have taken her into my confidence."

Mrs. Wilson directed at Barbara a glance so compelling that it was almost hypnotic.

Bab did not return her look or make any answer.

A little while later Barbara disappeared. She went back alone to Mr. Hamlin's study. On top of his desk she discovered a box about a foot and a half long. It had been opened and a key was lying beside it on the desk. Barbara could see that there was no money in the box, only a collection of papers. Bab returned the long envelope, which she had found at Mrs. Wilson's feet in the hall to its place, turned the key in the lock of the box, and then carried the key upstairs, intending to hand it over to Harriet. But Bab did not know whether or not she ought to explain to Harriet how she had come by the key.

Harriet was in the room with Mrs. Wilson, seeing her guest to bed for the second time, when Barbara went upstairs. Bab had no desire to face Mrs. Wilson again that night. The distrust of the woman that was deepening in the girl's mind was too great to conceal.

"Come into my room in the morning before breakfast, Harriet, dear," Mrs. Wilson entreated, as she kissed her young hostess good night. "I know you will forgive my foolishness, when I have had a little talk with you. It is too late now for explanations."

It was between two and three o'clock in the morning before the household of the Assistant Secretary of State again settled itself to sleep. Under her pillow Barbara Thurston had the key to Mr. William Hamlin's strong box, in which valuable state papers were sometimes temporarily placed.

CHAPTER XVIII

Harriet Hamlin spent half an hour in the room with Mrs. Wilson before she came down to the breakfast table the next morning.

"It is all right, girls," she announced promptly, as soon as the maid left the room. "Mrs. Wilson is going to have her breakfast in bed. She is a little upset by the happenings of last night. But she has explained everything to me. For some time, Mrs. Wilson has been trying to play a joke on Father, and last night she made another attempt. I promised her none of us would mention to him what had occurred. Will you give me your word, all of you, not to tell?"

"Certainly, Harriet," Ruth agreed seriously. The other three "Automobile Girls" quietly nodded their heads.

"I don't know that I quite approve of Mrs. Wilson's method of practical joking," Harriet went on. "She frightened all of us. But then, if no one had discovered her, no harm would have been done."

Mollie and Grace gazed at Harriet, without trying to conceal their surprise, but Ruth and Bab only looked steadfastly at their plates.

"Father is so strict and good all the time, I just wish somebody would play a trick on him," Harriet went on angrily. She was annoyed at the attitude of the "Automobile Girls," and she was still smarting under the hurt of her father's speech the night before. As long as her father had refused her money before she had even asked him for it, Harriet had decided that it would be worse than useless to appeal to him again. She was now waiting for disaster to break over her head.

"Mrs. Wilson rather blames you, Barbara," Harriet continued. "She says she did not succeed in her joke, after all, because you came down stairs at the wrong time and foiled the whole thing. She could not find the silly old paper she needed. But do please be quiet as mice about the whole affair. Don't mention it before the servants. Father will be home to-night. Will you girls mind excusing me for the day, and finding some way of amusing yourselves? I have promised Mrs. Wilson to go home with her."

"Of course we can get along, Harriet," Grace replied. "I hope you will have a good time."

Bab made no answer to Harriet's report of Mrs. Wilson's attitude toward her. But she was convinced that Mrs. Wilson knew she had discovered the stolen paper and returned it to its rightful place.

The "Automobile Girls" did not see Harriet again that morning.

At noon a message was sent upstairs. Mr. William Hamlin had returned and wished to see his daughter at once. When he learned that Harriet was not at home, he immediately sent for Ruth.

"Ruth, I have come home sooner than I had planned," he declared, "And I wish to have a talk with you. Now, please keep your self-control. Girls and women have such a fashion of flying into a rage at the first word one says, that it is perfectly impossible to have any reasonable conversation with them. I wish to talk with you quite quietly and calmly."

"Very well, Uncle," Ruth replied, meekly enough, though she was far from feeling meek. She could readily understand why Harriet had found it impossible to make a confidant of her father.

"I am glad you are so sensible, Ruth," Mr. Hamlin went on. "For I have reason to believe that your friend, Barbara Thurston, has proved herself an undesirable guest, since her arrival in Washington, which I very much deplore. She is dishonorable, for she has secretly entered my study and been seen handling my papers, and she has contracted a debt; for I saw the check by means of which she returned the borrowed money to Mrs. Wilson. I cannot understand how you and your father have managed to be so deceived by the young woman."

"Stop, Uncle William," Ruth interrupted hotly. "I cannot, of course, tell you that the things which you say are untrue. But at least I have the right to say that I positively know you are wrong. I shall ask Barbara to come down to your study, at once, to deny these charges. Then we shall go home immediately."

"There, Ruth, I expected it," Mr. Hamlin answered testily. "Just as I said. You have gone off the handle at once. Of course your young friend may have some plausible explanation for her actions. But I will not be guilty of making any accusations against a guest in my own house under any circumstances. I have only mentioned these facts to you because I feel that it is my positive duty to warn you against this girl, whom you have chosen for your most intimate friend. It is impossible that I have been deceived in regard to her. I have positive proof of what I say, and I sadly fear she is a very headstrong and misguided girl."

Ruth was already crying from anger, which made it hard for her to answer her uncle's speech. "You certainly don't object to my telling Barbara of your accusations, Uncle William?" Ruth demanded. "I think it is only fair to her."

"Not while she is in my house. You are to tell her nothing," Mr. Hamlin ordered. "When Miss Thurston leaves you may tell her whatever you wish. But I will not have a scene with her while she is staying here."

Mr. Hamlin was a cold, selfish and arrogant man. He well deserved the blow to his pride that he was to receive later.

Ruth controlled herself in order to think deeply and quietly. Her father was wise in his trust in her. Ruth had excellent judgment and good sense. She was not particularly impressed by her uncle's command. She felt that she had a perfect right to tell her friend of what she had been accused. Yet would it be a good idea? Barbara would be heart-broken, and nothing would induce her to remain in Mr. Hamlin's house another hour after she learned his opinion of her. Ruth knew it would not be well for Bab to rush off home in sudden anger, leaving a false impression behind her. Barbara must stay in Mr. Hamlin's house until he himself apologized to her.

Ruth did not dare to go back upstairs to the other girls immediately after her interview with her uncle. She knew her friends would recognize at once, from her red eyes and her excitement, that something was the matter. Yet Ruth longed for a confidant, and she meant to unburden herself to Grace as soon as she had the opportunity. To go upstairs now would reveal everything to Mollie and Barbara as well.

Ruth seized her coat and hat from a closet in the hall and rushed out into the street. She began walking as rapidly as she could, to let the fresh air cool the tumult of feeling that was surging within her. Ruth must have walked a mile before she determined what to do. Before she returned to Mr. Hamlin's house, she found a telegraph office and went into it. She sent a telegram to her father in Chicago, which read:

"Come to Washington as soon as possible. Bab wrongly suspected. She is still in ignorance, but we need you.

"Ruth Stuart."

Little did Ruth yet dream why these toils were being wound about unhappy Barbara. Mollie's one act of weakness had involved her sister in a number of actions that did look wrong to an outsider. Yet the explanation of them was so simple, if Bab had only known it were best for her to tell the whole story! But Barbara was trying to shield Mollie, and Mollie did not dream that Bab would suffer any consequences from her foolish deed. So Bab's peculiar proceedings since her arrival in Washington had indeed played well into the hands of her enemies. Mr. Hamlin's mind had been poisoned against her. She had been seen to do several underhanded things, one following directly after the other. If a big game were being attempted, the reputation of Barbara Thurston was of little account. Besides Bab had already blocked several of the players in the game. Revenge could very well enter into the present scheme of things, and a girl who had no one to defend her might prove a useful tool. As a last resort she could be made a scapegoat.

In the meanwhile, Barbara was blissfully unconscious of any trouble, and went singing cheerily about her room that morning. Since the delivery of her check to Mrs. Wilson it seemed to her that the skies were blue again. During the rest of her stay in Washington Bab meant just to enjoy the beautiful sights of the wonderful city and not to trouble about the disagreeable people. She did intend to ask Harriet to take her to see the cunning little Chinese girl, Wee Tu, before she went home, but she had no other very definite desires.

As for Mrs. Wilson? Barbara had just wisely decided that the woman belonged to a curious type, which she did not understand and wished to keep away from. Bab did not admire Mrs. Wilson's methods of playing jokes. On the other hand it was none of Barbara Thurston's business. So long as she had put the paper back in Mr. Hamlin's strong box no harm had been done.

Barbara still had in her possession the key to that strong box. She had neglected to give it to Harriet, because Harriet had left home so soon after breakfast. And now that very terrifying person, Mr. William Hamlin, had returned home, and Barbara Thurston still had the key in her possession. Even Ruth had gone out. What should she do? She decided to keep the key until Harriet came back in the afternoon. Then Harriet could make some sort of explanation to her father. Barbara simply did not have the courage to tell Mr. Hamlin that she had discovered Mrs. Wilson tampering with his papers, and that it was she who had found the stolen paper and locked it up again.

However, fate was certainly against Bab at the present time. A servant knocked at the door of the next room, where Grace and Mollie were reading.

"Please," the maid said, "Mr. Hamlin wants to know if Miss Harriet left a key with you? It is a most important key, and Mr. Hamlin needs it at once."

Grace and Mollie both shook their heads. No; Harriet had mentioned no such key to them. Barbara was waiting in the next room with the door open. She knew her turn would come next.

"Do you know anything of the key, Miss Barbara?" Harriet's maid inquired.

Of course Bab blushed. She always did at the wrong time.

"Yes, I have the key, Mary," she replied. "Wait a minute, I will get it for you."

"Do the young ladies know anything of my key?" Mr. William Hamlin's impatient voice was heard just outside Barbara's door.

Innocently the maid opened it. "Wait a minute, Mr. Hamlin, please. Miss Thurston says she has the key. She is getting it for you now."

And Barbara had to come to the door herself to present the key to this dreadful old "Bluebeard."

"I presume my daughter left my key in your charge," Mr. Hamlin asked coldly.

"No," she declared almost under her breath, hoping her stern host would either not hear her, or at least not heed her. "Harriet did not leave it with me."

"Then kindly tell me how my key came into your possession?" Mr. Hamlin inquired, in chilling, even tones. Bab shivered.

"I found it," Bab answered lamely, having it in mind to tell the whole strange story of last night's experience. But she was too frightened by Mr. Hamlin's manner and by the fear that she would be regarded as a telltale by Harriet. If Mr. Hamlin's own daughter had not considered her guest's actions unusual, it was not exactly Bab's place to report them. So she remained silent, and her host also turned away in silence.

Harriet did not come home until just before dinner time. She told the "Automobile Girls" she had spent a delightful day, but her behavior was unusual. She looked frightened, though at the same time happier than she had seemed since the hour she had received the first threatening letter from her dressmaker.

Peter Dillon had walked home with Harriet. Barbara, who happened to be standing at the front window, saw them stop to talk for a moment at the door before Peter said good-bye. Peter was making himself very charming to Harriet. He was talking to her in his half laughing, half earnest fashion in the very manner that had seemed so attractive to Bab, too, at first. But it was a manner she had learned later on to distrust and even to fear.

When Harriet parted from Peter Dillon she nodded her head emphatically and apparently made him a promise, and Barbara saw Peter look back at her with a peculiar smile as she ascended the steps.

CHAPTER XIX

Harriet Hamlin was restless and nervous all the next day. Even Mr. Hamlin, noticing his daughter's nervous manner at luncheon, suggested that she take her friends out to pay some calls. So Bab put forth her plea that she wished to make another visit to the home of the Chinese minister. As the girls had not yet paid their luncheon call at the embassy Harriet agreed to take them to see Wee Tu. Before she left the house Harriet called up her dressmaker and had a long confidential talk with her over the telephone. She seemed in better spirits afterwards.

The Chinese minister's wife, Lady Tu, was receiving. As there were no men in the drawing-room, her daughter, Wee Tu, sat among the young girls as quiet and demure as a picture on a fan.

Bab managed to persuade the little girl into a corner to have a quiet chat with her. But Miss Wee Tu was difficult to draw out. Across the room, Harriet Hamlin chanced to mention the name of Peter Dillon. At once the little Chinese girl's expression changed. The change was very slight. Hardly a shade of emotion crossed her unexpressive, Oriental face, but curious Barbara was watching for that very change. She remembered the young girl had been affected by Peter's appearance during their former visit.

"Do you like Mr. Dillon?" inquired Bab. She had no excuse for her question except her own wilful curiosity.

But Wee Tu was not to be caught napping.

"Lige?" she answered, with a soft rising inflection that made the "k" in "like" sound as "g." "I do not know what Americans mean by the word—'Lige.' You 'lige' so many people. A Chinese girl 'liges' only a few—her parents, her relatives; sometimes she 'liges' her husband, but not always."

"Don't like your husband!" exclaimed Bab in surprise. "Why, what do you mean?"

The little Chinese maiden was confused both by the American word and the American idea.

"The Chinese girl has respect for her husband; she does what he tells her to do, but she does not all the time 'lige' him, because her father has chosen him for her husband. I shall marry a prince, when I go back to China, but he is 'verra' old."

"Oh, I see!" Bab rejoined. "You thought I meant 'love' when I said 'like.' It is quite different to love a person." Bab smiled wisely. "To love is to like a great deal."

"Then I love this Mr. Peter Dillon," said the Chinese girl sweetly.

Bab gasped in shocked surprise.

"It is most improper that I say so, is it not?" smiled Miss Wee Tu. "But so many things that American girls do seem improper to Chinese ladies. And I do like this Mr. Peter very much. He comes always to our house. He is 'verra' intimate with my father. He talks to him a long, long time and they have Chinese secrets together. Then he talks with me so that I can understand him. Many people will not trouble with a Chinese girl, who is only fifteen, even if her father is a minister."

Barbara was overwhelmed with Wee Tu's confidence, but she knew she deserved it as a punishment for her curiosity. The strangest thing was that the young Chinese girl spoke in a low, even voice, without the least change of expression in her long, almond eyes. Any one watching her would have thought she was talking of the weather.

"I go back to China when my father's time in the United States is over and then I get married. It makes no difference. But while I am in your country I play I am free, like an American girl, and I do what I like inside my own head."

"It's very wrong," Barbara argued hastily. "It is much better to trust to your parents."

"Yes?" answered Wee Tu quietly. Bab was vexed that Peter Dillon's careless Irish manners had also charmed this little Oriental maiden. But Bab was wise enough to understand that Wee Tu's interest was only that of a child who was grateful to the young man for his kindness.

Barbara rose to join her friends, who were at this moment saying good-bye to their hostess.

"It is the Chinese custom," Lady Tu remarked graciously, "to make little presents to our guests. Will not Mr. Hamlin's daughter and her four friends receive these poor offerings?"

A servant handed the girls five beautiful, carved tortoise shell boxes, containing exquisite sets of combs for their hair, the half dozen or more that Chinese women wear.

"I felt ashamed of my wind-blown hair when Lady Tu presented us with these combs," Grace exclaimed, just before the little party reached home. They had paid a dozen more calls since their visit to the Chinese Embassy. "I suppose Chinese women are shocked at the way American girls wear their hair."

"Yes, but we can't take three hours to fix ours," laughed Mollie, running up the steps of the Hamlin house. In the front hall Mollie spied an immense box of roses. They were for Harriet. Harriet picked up the box languidly and started upstairs. She had talked very little during the afternoon, and had seemed unlike herself.

"Aren't you going to open your flowers, Harriet?" Mollie pleaded. "I am crazy to see them."

"I'll open them if it pleases you, Mollie," Harriet returned gently. The great box was crowded with long-stemmed American beauties and violets.

"Have some posies, girls?" Harriet said generously, holding out her arms filled with flowers. For a long time afterwards the "Automobile Girls" remembered how beautiful Harriet looked as she stood there, her face very pale, her black hair and hat outlined against the dark oak woodwork with the great bunch of American beauties in her arms.

"Of course we don't want your posies, Lady Harriet," Mollie answered affectionately. "Here is the note to tell you who sent them to you." But Harriet went on to her room without showing enough interest in her gift to open the letter.

After dinner Harriet complained of a headache, and went immediately to her room. The "Automobile Girls" were going out to a theater party, which was being given in their honor by their old friends, Mrs. Post and Hugh. Harriet sent word she would have to be excused. When Ruth put her head into Harriet's room to say good-bye, just before she started for the theater, she thought she heard her cousin crying.

"Harriet, dear, do let me stay with you," Ruth pleaded. "I am afraid you are feeling worse than you will let us know."

But Harriet insisted that she desired only to be left alone. Feeling strangely unhappy about her cousin, Ruth, at last joined the theater party.

Mr. Hamlin did not leave the house immediately after dinner, although he had an engagement to spend the evening at the home of Mrs. Wilson. She had asked him, only that morning, to come. Mr. Hamlin was also troubled about his daughter. He had not been so unobservant that he had not seen the change in her. She was less animated, less talkative. Mr. Hamlin feared Harriet was not well. Though he was stern and unsympathetic with Harriet, he was genuinely frightened if she were in the least ill.

So it was with unusual gentleness that he tapped lightly on Harriet's door.

"I am all right, Mary, thank you," Harriet replied, believing her maid to be outside. "Go to bed whenever you please. I shall fall asleep after a while."

Mr. Hamlin cleared his throat and Harriet started nervously. Why was her father standing outside her door? Had he learned of her bill to her dressmaker?

"I do not wish to disturb you, Harriet," Mr. Hamlin began awkwardly. "I only desired to know if I could do anything for you."

"No, Father," poor Harriet replied wearily. As Mr. Hamlin turned away, she sprang up and started to run after him. At her own door she stopped. She heard her father's stern voice giving an order to a servant, and her sudden resolution died within her. A few moments later the front door closed behind him and her opportunity had passed.

An hour afterwards, when the house was quiet and the servants nowhere about, Harriet Hamlin slipped cautiously downstairs. She was gone only a few minutes. But when she came back to her own room, she opened a private drawer in her bureau and hid something in it. Harriet then threw herself on her bed and lay for a long time with her eyes wide open, staring straight ahead of her.

Just before midnight, when she heard the gay voices of her friends returning from the theater, and when Ruth tripped softly to her bedroom, Harriet lay with closed eyes, apparently fast asleep.

The next morning Harriet was really ill. Her hand trembled so while she poured the breakfast coffee that she spilled some of it on the tablecloth. When Mr. Hamlin spoke to her sharply she burst into tears and left the room, leaving her father ashamed of himself, and the "Automobile Girls" so embarrassed that they ate the rest of their breakfast in painful silence. Ruth did dart one indignant glance at her uncle, which Mr. Hamlin saw, but did not in his heart resent.

Harriet was willing, that morning, to have Ruth come into her darkened bedroom and sit by her bed. For Harriet's wakeful night had left her slightly feverish.

"I don't want to disturb you, Harriet," Bab apologized, coming softly to the door. "But some one has just telephoned for you. The person at the telephone has a message for you, but whoever it is refuses to give his name. What shall I do!"

Harriet sat up in bed, quickly, a hunted expression on her beautiful face. "Tell Mr. Peter Dillon that I will keep my word," Harriet answered angrily. "He is not to worry about me again."

"Is that your message?" Bab queried wonderingly. "It was not Mr.

Dillon's voice."

Harriet laughed hysterically. "Of course not!" she returned. "Oh, I know you girls are wondering why I am behaving so strangely. And I am breaking my word to tell you. But I must tell some one. I don't care what Mrs. Wilson and Peter Dillon say, I know I can trust you. I have decided to help Mrs. Wilson and Peter play their silly joke on Father and the State Department! Oh, you needn't look so horrified, girls. It is only a joke. The papers are about some Chinese business. I have them hid in my bureau drawer."

Harriet nodded toward her dressing-table, while Ruth and Bab stood looking at each other, speechless with horror, the same idea growing in their minds.

"When Father comes to look for his stupid papers he'll find them gone, and, of course, will think he has misplaced them," Harriet continued. "He will be dreadfully worried for a little while; then Mrs. Wilson will return the papers to me and I will slip them back in their old place, and Father will never know what has happened. Mrs. Wilson and Peter have vowed they will never betray me, and I have promised not to betray them. If I were to be caught, I suppose Father would never forgive me. But I'll take good care that he doesn't find out about it."

"Harriet, do please give up this foolish plan!" Ruth entreated earnestly. "I know you are doing something wrong. Mrs. Wilson and Mr. Dillon both know that Uncle William's papers are too valuable to be played with. Why, they belong to the United States Government, not to him! Harriet, I implore you, do not touch your father's papers!"

Harriet shook her head obstinately. She was absolutely adamant. Ruth pleaded, scolded, in vain. Bab did not say a word nor enter a protest. She was too frightened. All of a sudden a veil had been rent asunder. Now she believed she understood what Peter Dillon and Mrs. Wilson had planned from the beginning. They were spies in the service of some higher power. The papers that Harriet thought were to be used for a joke on her father were really to be sold! Was not some state secret to be betrayed? Ever since Bab's arrival in Washington it had looked as though Peter Dillon and Mrs. Wilson had been working toward this very end. Having failed with her they had turned their attention to poor Harriet. But Mrs. Wilson and Peter Dillon must be only hired tools! Shrewdly Barbara Thurston recalled her recent conversation with innocent Wee Tu: "Mr. Dillon and my father, they have Chinese secrets together." Could a certain distinguished and wisely silent Oriental gentleman be responsible for the thrilling drama about to be enacted? Bab was never to know positively, and she wisely kept her suspicion to herself.

"I do wish, Ruth, you and Bab would go away and leave me alone," Harriet protested. "I shall be well enough to get up for luncheon, if you will let me take a nap. I don't see any harm in playing this joke on Father. At any rate, I have quite made up my mind to go through with my part in it and I won't give up my plan. You can tell Father if you choose, of course. I cannot prevent that. I know I was foolish to have confided in you. But, unless you are despicable tale bearers, the papers in my bureau drawer will go out of this house in a few hours! I don't see any harm in their disappearing for a little while. Father will have them back in a few days. Please go!"

Yet with all Harriet's air of bravado, however, there was one point in her story which she did not mention. In return for her delivery of certain of her father's state papers Mrs. Wilson and Peter Dillon had promised to advance to Harriet the five hundred dollars necessary to pay her dressmaker. Harriet had agreed only to receive it as a loan. And she tried to comfort herself with the idea that her friends were only doing her a kindness in exchange for the favor she was to do for them. Still, the thought of the money worried Harriet. But how else was she to be saved from the weight of her stern father's displeasure?

CHAPTER XX

At Harriet's request Bab and Ruth went silently out of her room, their faces white and frightened.

"Ruth, is there any place where we can be alone?" Barbara whispered faintly. "I must talk with you."

Ruth nodded, and the two friends found their way into the library, turning the key in the lock. Then they stood facing each other, speechless, for a moment, from the very intensity of their feelings.

"Ruth, you must do something," Bab entreated. "The papers that Mrs. Wilson and Mr. Dillon are making Harriet get for them they do not intend to use for a joke. Oh, Ruth, they are no doubt important state papers! Harriet may be betraying her country and ruining her father by placing these papers in their hands."

"I think, too, that Mrs. Wilson and Peter Dillon are spies," Ruth returned more quietly. "And, of course, we must do something to prevent their getting their hands on the papers."

"But what can we do?" Barbara demanded sharply. "We cannot tell Mr. Hamlin of Harriet's deed. It would be too cruel of us. Nor can we confront Mrs. Wilson and Peter Dillon with the accusation. They would only laugh at us, and declare that we were mad to have imagined any such thing. Then, again, we would be betraying Harriet's confidence. We do not know just what state papers Harriet is to give to them, but they must be very, very valuable. I suppose those dreadful people will have the papers copied, sell our country's secret, and return the papers to Harriet when all the mischief has been done. Ruth, I believe, now, that Mrs. Wilson and Peter Dillon both meant to make me steal Mr. Hamlin's papers. Then they would have declared I had sold them to some one. And Mr. Hamlin would never have suspected his friends. Now, they think poor Harriet will be too much afraid to betray them."

Bab's voice trembled slightly. She realized how nearly she had been the dupe of these two clever schemers. She felt that she and Ruth must save Harriet at all events.

"Mrs. Wilson tried to steal Mr. Hamlin's papers the night she masqueraded as a ghost," Barbara continued. "I picked up the envelope she dropped on the floor in the hall."

"I know it, Barbara," Ruth answered in her self-controlled fashion, which always had a calming effect on the more impetuous Bab. "I also believe Mrs. Wilson meant to fix the guilt of the theft upon you. Uncle William called me into his study the other day and asked me if I considered you trustworthy. Of course I was awfully indignant and told him just what I thought of him for being so suspicious. But I believe Mrs. Wilson had tried to poison his mind against you. You must be on your guard now, Bab, dear. If Harriet gives up these papers of Uncle's the plotters may still try to use you as their scapegoat. When Uncle finds his papers have disappeared Mrs. Wilson and Mr. Dillon will, of course, appear to know nothing of them; but they will somehow try to direct suspicion against you, trusting to Harriet's cowardice. Don't you worry though, Bab, dear. You shall not suffer for Harriet's fault while I am here."

"Oh, I am not worrying about myself, Ruth," Bab answered. "It is Harriet's part in the affair that troubles me. Do, please, go to Harriet and talk to her again. Surely you can make her see the risk she is running. Do you suppose it would do any good if I were to call on Mrs. Wilson? I could just pretend I still thought she meant to play the joke on Mr. Hamlin. You know she told me she intended to do so. I could beg her to give it up without mentioning Harriet's name or letting Mrs. Wilson guess that Harriet had confided in us."

Ruth shook her head. "It would not do any good for you to go to Mrs. Wilson, Bab. And, somehow, I am afraid for you. We do not know how much further they intend to involve you in their plot."

"Oh, they won't do me any harm, now," Barbara rejoined. "Anyhow, I am willing to take the risk, if Harriet will not give in."

"Just wait here, Bab, until I have been to see Harriet again," Ruth entreated. "I will go down on my knees to her, if I can persuade her to give up this wicked deed. Oh, why is she so determined to be so reckless and so foolish?"

Fifteen minutes afterwards Ruth came back from her second interview with Harriet, looking utterly discouraged. "Harriet simply won't give up," Ruth reported to Bab. "She is absolutely determined to go her own way, and she is angry with me for interfering. Oh, Bab, what will happen? Uncle is so proud! If his daughter is known to have given Mrs. Wilson and Peter Dillon state papers, the report will be circulated that she stole them, and Uncle William will be disgraced. Then, what will become of Harriet? She does not intend to do wrong. But I simply can't make her see this thing as we see it. So what can we do?" Unusually self-contained, Ruth broke down, now, weeping on Bab's shoulder. The thought of the dreadful disgrace to her uncle and her cousin was more than she could face.

"I am going to see Mrs. Wilson, Ruth," Bab declared. "You had better stay here and do your best with Harriet. The papers are not to be delivered until four this afternoon, when, I believe, Harriet is to meet Peter Dillon. Of course it was he who telephoned Harriet, only he was clever enough to disguise his voice. So we have until afternoon to work. Don't worry yourself sick. We simply must save Harriet in some way. I don't pretend that I see the way clearly yet, but I have faith that it will come. I cannot do any harm by going to Mrs. Wilson, and I may do some good."

"I don't like you to go there alone, Bab," Ruth faltered. "But I don't dare to leave Harriet by herself. She might find a way to give up the papers while we were out, and then all would be lost!"

When Bab rang the bell at the door of Mrs. Wilson's home she did not know that her approach had been watched. She meant to be very careful during her interview, for she realized that she and Ruth were endeavoring to foil two brilliant and unscrupulous enemies.

Mrs. Wilson and Peter were in the library, and through the window Mrs. Wilson had watched Bab approaching the house.

"Here comes that tiresome Thurston girl, whom you were going to use as your tool, Peter," teased Mrs. Wilson. "She wasn't so easy to manage as you thought, was she? Never mind; she will still be used as our scapegoat. But I shall not see her this morning. What's the use?"

"Let her come in, by all means, Mrs. Wilson," Peter Dillon urged. "I shall hide so that she will not see me. What would fall in with our plans better than to have this girl come here to-day! Who knows how this visit may be made to count against her? Of course, if suspicion never points to us we had best never mention the name of Barbara Thurston. But—if Mr. Hamlin ever questions you, why not say Miss Thurston came here to-day and betrayed the fact to you that she had stolen Mr. Hamlin's papers? We have circumstantial evidence enough against her."

Bab found Mrs. Wilson very much surprised to see her, and looking very languid and bored. Straightforward Barbara rushed headlong into her request.

"Really, Miss Thurston, don't you think you are rather impertinent?" drawled her hostess, when Bab finished. "I don't see what business it is of yours whether or not I wish to play a joke on my friend, Mr. Hamlin. Don't try to get out of mischief by reporting to Mr. Hamlin the story of my poor little joke. You can hardly save yourself by any such method. No one will believe you. And I have an idea that you came to my house to-day for a very different purpose than to persuade me to give up my joke. What was it?"

Bab was mystified. She had no idea how Mrs. Wilson and Peter Dillon had planned to use her visit as evidence against her, so it was impossible for her to understand Mrs. Wilson's insinuation.

Barbara did not stay long. She saw Mrs. Wilson had no intention of being persuaded from her design. Even though the woman was beginning to see that Bab and Ruth were a little suspicious of her, she had no idea of being frightened from her deep-laid scheme by two insignificant schoolgirls.

Barbara hurried to her car as fast as she could, anxious to get back to Ruth and to devise some other move to checkmate the traitors. She even hoped, against hope, that Harriet had been induced to change her mind and that all would yet be well. But as Bab jumped aboard her car she saw another girl, running down the street, waving something in the air and evidently trying to induce Bab's street car to wait for her. Barbara begged the conductor to hold the car for a moment, before she recognized the figure, running toward them. But the next second she beheld the ever-present newspaper girl, Marjorie Moore, tablet and pencil in hand, completely out of breath and exhausted. Marjorie Moore could not speak for some time after she had secured a seat next Bab in the car.

"I have been watching Mrs. Wilson's house since eight o'clock this morning," she finally gasped. "What on earth made you go in there?"

"I can't tell you," Bab returned coldly. Not for anything in the world would she have Marjorie Moore suspect what she and Ruth feared.

Miss Moore gave a little, half amused, half sarcastic laugh. "You can't tell? Oh, never mind, my dear. I know you are all right. You weren't doing anything wrong. I expect you were trying to help set matters straight. You don't need to tell me anything. I think I know all that is necessary. Good-bye now. I must get off this car at the corner. Let me tell you, however, not to worry, whatever happens. I am in possession of all the facts, so there will be no trouble in proving them. But if anything disagreeable happens to you," Marjorie Moore gave Bab a reassuring smile, "telephone me, will you? My number is 1607, Union."

Marjorie Moore rushed out of the street car as hurriedly as she had entered it, before Bab could take in what she had said.

Barbara puzzled all the rest of the way home. Could it be possible that Marjorie Moore had discovered Mrs. Wilson's and Peter's plot? Could she also have guessed Harriet's part in it? Bab shuddered, for she remembered the newspaper girl's words to her on the night of their first meeting: "If ever I have a chance to get even with Harriet Hamlin, won't I take my revenge?" Did Marjorie Moore also suspect that an effort would be made to draw Barbara into this whirlpool of disgrace?

No one ate any luncheon at the home of the Assistant Secretary of State, except Mollie and Grace. Fortunately Mr. Hamlin did not return home. Ruth and Bab had decided not to tell the other two "Automobile Girls" of their terrible uneasiness unless they actually needed the help of the younger girls to save the situation. Ruth and Bab did not wish to prejudice Mollie and Grace against Harriet if it were possible to spare her. But Ruth had told Bab that, at four o'clock, Harriet was determined to deliver the papers to Peter Dillon.

At two o'clock, however, the two friends had found no way to influence Harriet to give up her mad project. Indeed, Harriet scarcely spoke to either of them, she was so bitterly angry at what she termed their interference.

At three o'clock, Ruth and Barbara grew desperate. For, at three, Harriet Hamlin closed the door of her bedroom and commenced to dress for her engagement.

"Try once again, Ruth," Bab pleaded. "It is worse even than you know. I believe Marjorie Moore suspects what Harriet is about to do. Suppose she publishes the story in the morning papers. Tell Harriet I have a reason for thinking she knows about the affair."

Bab waited apprehensively for Ruth's return. It seemed to her that, for the first time in their adventures, the "Automobile Girls" had met with a situation that no amount of pluck or effort on their part could control. This was the most important experience of their whole lives, for their country was about to be betrayed! Once Barbara stamped her foot in her impatience. How dared Harriet Hamlin be so willful, so headstrong? Bab's face was white with anxiety and suspense. Her lips twitched nervously. Then in a flash her whole expression changed. The color came back to her cheeks, the light to her eyes. At the eleventh hour the way had been made clear.

Ruth had no such look when she returned to Barbara. She flung herself despondently into a chair. "It's no use," she declared despairingly. "Harriet must go her own way. We can do nothing with her!"

"Yes, we can!" Bab whispered. She leaned over and murmured something in Ruth's ear.

Ruth sprang to her feet. "Barbara Thurston, you are perfectly wonderful!" she cried. "Yes, I do know where it is. Go to my desk and take that blank paper. It is just the right size. Fold it up in three parts. There, it will do, now; give it to me. Now go and command Grace and Mollie, if they love us, to call Harriet out of her room for a minute. We can explain to them afterwards."

Mollie and Grace feared Barbara had gone suddenly mad when she rushed in upon them with her demand. But Mollie did manage to persuade Harriet to go into the next room. As Harriet slipped out of her bedroom, her cousin, Ruth Stuart, stole into it, hiding something she held in her hand. She was alone in Harriet's room for not more than two minutes.

At a quarter to four o'clock, Harriet Hamlin left her father's house with a large envelope concealed inside her shopping bag. Opposition had merely strengthened Harriet's original resolution. She was no longer frightened. Ruth and Bab were absurd to have been so tragic over a silly joke.

At a little after four o'clock, in a quiet, out-of-the-way street in Washington, Harriet turned over to Peter Dillon this envelope, which, as she supposed, contained the much-coveted papers which she had extracted from the private collection of the Assistant Secretary of State.

Whatever the papers were, Peter Dillon took them carelessly with his usual charming smile. But inwardly he was chanting a song of victory. He and Mrs. Wilson would be many-thousands of dollars richer by this time to-morrow. He glanced into the envelope with his near-sighted eyes. The papers were folded up inside and all was well! Peter did not dare, before Harriet, to be too interested in what the envelope contained.

It would not have made him happier to have looked closer; the song of victory would have died away on his lips. For, instead of certain secret documents sent to the office of the Secretary of State, from representatives of the United States Government in China, Harriet Hamlin had turned over to Peter Dillon an official envelope, which contained only folded sheets of blank paper!

It had been Barbara's idea and Ruth had carried it out successfully. In the moment when Harriet left her room in answer to Mollie's call, Ruth had exchanged the valuable state papers for the worthless ones. Once Harriet was safely out of the way, she and Bab carried the precious documents downstairs and shut them up in Mr. Hamlin's desk. Both girls hoped that all trouble was now averted, and that Mr. Hamlin would never hear of Harriet's folly!

CHAPTER XXI

The members of the Hamlin household went early to their own rooms that night.

Ruth at once flung herself down on a couch without removing her clothing. In a few minutes she was fast asleep, for she believed their difficulties were over. Bab did not feel as secure. She was still thinking of the speech the newspaper girl had made to her in the car.

At ten o'clock the Assistant Secretary of State, who was sitting alone in his study, heard a violent ringing of his telephone bell. He did not know that, at this same instant, his daughter Harriet had crept down to his study door intending to make a full confession of her mistakes to him.

Mr. Hamlin picked up the receiver. "'The Washington News?' Yes. You have something important to say to me? Well, what is it?" Mr. Hamlin listened quietly for a little while. Then Harriet heard him cry in a hoarse, unnatural voice: "Impossible! The thing is preposterous! Where did you ever get hold of such an absurd idea?"

Harriet stopped to listen no longer. She never knew how she got back upstairs to her room. She half staggered, half fell up the steps. Suddenly she realized everything! She had been used as a tool by Mrs. Wilson and Peter Dillon. Ruth and Barbara had been right. She had stolen her father's state papers. A newspaper had gotten hold of the story and already her father and she were disgraced.

In the meantime, Mr. Hamlin continued to talk over the telephone, though his hand shook so he was hardly able to hold the receiver.

"You say you think it best to warn me that the story of the theft of my papers will be published in the morning paper, that you know that private state documents entrusted to me keeping have been sold to secret spies? What evidence have you? I have missed no such papers. Wait a minute." Mr. Hamlin went to his strong box. Sure enough, certain documents were missing. Ruth and Bab had put the papers in the desk. "Have you an idea who stole my papers?" Mr. Hamlin called back over the telephone wire, his voice shaken with passion.

Evidently the editor who was talking to Mr. Hamlin now lost his courage. He did not dare to tell Mr. Hamlin that his own daughter was suspected of having sold her father's papers. Mr. Hamlin repeated the editor's exact words. "You say a young woman sold my papers? You are right; this is not a matter to be discussed over the telephone. Send some one up from your office to see me at once."

Mr. Hamlin reeled over to his bell-rope and gave it a pull, so that the noise of its ringing sounded like an alarm through the quiet house.

A frightened servant answered the bell.

"Tell Miss Thurston and my niece, Miss Stuart, to come to my study at once," Mr. Hamlin ordered. The man-servant obeyed.

"Ruth, dear, wake up," Bab entreated, giving her friend a shake. "Something awful must have happened. Your uncle has sent for us. He must have missed those papers."

[Illustration: "What Have You Done With My Papers?"]

Ruth and Bab, both of them looking unutterably miserable and shaken, entered Mr. Hamlin's study. Their host did not speak as they first approached him. When he did he turned on them such a haggard, wretched face that they were filled with pity. But the instant Mr. Hamlin caught sight of Barbara his expression changed. He took her by the arm, and, before she could guess what was going to happen, he shook her violently.

"What have you done with my state papers?" he demanded. "Tell me quickly. Don't hesitate. There may yet be time to save us both. Oh, I should never have let you stay in this house!" he groaned. "I suspected you of mischief when I learned of your first visit to my office. But I did not believe such treachery could be found in a young girl. Ruth, can't you make your friend speak! If she will tell me to whom she sold my papers, I will forgive her everything! But I must know where they are at once. I can then force the newspaper to keep silence and force my enemies to return me the documents, if there is only time!"

Barbara dropped into a chair and covered her face with her hands. She did not utter a word of reproach to Mr. Hamlin for his cruel suspicion of her. She could not tell him that his daughter Harriet was the real thief.

"Uncle," Ruth entreated, laying a quiet hand on Mr. Hamlin's arm, "listen to me for a moment. Yes, you must listen! You are not disgraced; you are not ruined. Look in your desk. Your papers are still there. Only the old envelope is gone. I put the papers in this drawer only this afternoon, because I did not know in what place you kept them. Some papers were given away, a few hours ago, to two people, whom you believed to be your friends, to Mrs. Wilson and Peter Dillon. But they were not your state papers, they were only blank sheets."

Mr. Hamlin looked into his drawer and saw the lost documents, then he passed his hand over his forehead. "I don't understand," he muttered. "Do you mean that, instead of the actual papers, you saved me by substituting blank papers for these valuable ones? Then your friend did try to sell her country's secrets, and you saved her and me. I shall never cease to be grateful to you to the longest day I live. For your sake I will spare your friend. But she must leave my house in the morning. I do not wish ever to look upon her again."

"Bab did not sell your papers, Uncle," Ruth protested passionately. "You shall not make such accusations against her. It was she who saved you. I did only what she told me to do. I did substitute the papers, but it was Barbara who thought of it."

"Then who, in Heaven's name, is guilty of this dreadful act?" Mr. Hamlin cried.

Neither Ruth nor Bab answered. Bab still sat with her face covered with her hands, in order to hide her hot tears. She cried partly for poor Harriet, and partly because of her sympathy for Mr. Hamlin. Ruth gazed at her uncle, white, silent and trembling.

"Who, Ruth? I demand to know!" Mr. Hamlin repeated.

"I shall not tell you," Ruth returned, with a little gasp.

"Send for my daughter, Harriet. She may know something," Mr. Hamlin ejaculated. Then he rang for a servant.

The two girls and the one man, who had grown old in the last few minutes, waited in unbroken silence. The girls had a strong desire to scream, to cry out, to warn Harriet. She must not let her father know of her foolish deed while his anger was at its height.

It seemed an eternity before the butler returned to Mr. Hamlin's study.

"Miss Hamlin is not in her room," he reported respectfully.

"Not in her room? Then look for her through the house," Mr. Hamlin repeated more quietly. He had gained greater control of himself. But a new fear was oppressing him, weighing him down. He would not give the idea credence even in his own mind.

Three—four—five minutes passed. Still Harriet did not appear.

"Let me look for Harriet, Uncle," Ruth implored, unable to control herself any longer.

At this moment Mollie came innocently down the stairs. "Is Mr. Hamlin looking for Harriet?" she inquired. "Harriet left the house ten minutes ago. She had on her coat and her hat, but she would not stop to say good-bye. I think her maid went with her. Mary had just a shawl thrown over her head. I am sure they will be back in a few minutes. Harriet must have gone out to post a letter. I thought she would have come back before this."

Imagine poor Mollie's horror and surprise when Mr. Hamlin dropped into a chair at her news and groaned: "It was Harriet after all. It was my own child!"

"Uncle, rouse yourself!" Ruth implored him. "Harriet thought she was only playing a harmless trick on you. She did not dream that the papers were of any importance. Mrs. Wilson and Peter Dillon deceived her cruelly. You must go and find out what has become of Harriet." Mr. Hamlin shook his head drearily.

"You must go!" insisted gentle Ruth, bursting into tears. "Harriet does not even know that the papers she gave away were worthless. If she has found out she has been duped she will be doubly desperate."

At this instant the door bell rang loudly. No one in the study appeared to hear it. Mollie had crept slowly back upstairs to Grace. Ruth, Mr. Hamlin and Bab were too wretched to stir.

A sound of hasty footsteps came down the hall, followed by a knock at the study door. The door flew open of its own accord. Like a vision straight from Heaven appeared the faces of Mr. Robert Stuart and his sister, Miss Sallie!

Ruth sprang into her father's arms with a cry of joy. And Bab, her eyes still streaming with tears, was caught up in the comforting arms of Miss Sallie.

CHAPTER XXII

"What does all this mean, William Hamlin?" Mr. Stuart inquired without ceremony.

With bowed head Mr. Hamlin told the whole story, not attempting to excuse himself, for Mr. Hamlin was a just man, though a severe one. He declared that he had been influenced to suspect Barbara ever since her arrival in his home. His enemies had also made a dupe of him, but his punishment had come upon him swiftly. He had just discovered that his own daughter had tried to deliver into the hands of paid spies, state papers of the United States Government.

Mr. Stuart and Aunt Sallie looked extremely serious while Mr. Hamlin was telling his story. But when Mr. Hamlin explained how Ruth and Bab had exchanged the valuable political documents for folded sheets of blank paper, Mr. Stuart burst into a loud laugh, and his expression changed as though by a miracle. He patted his daughter's shoulder to express his approval, while Miss Sallie kissed Bab with a sigh of relief.

Mr. Stuart and his sister had both been extremely uneasy since the arrival of Ruth's singular telegram, not knowing what troubled waters might be surrounding their "Automobile Girls." Indeed Miss Sallie had insisted on accompanying her brother to Washington, as she felt sure her presence would help to set things right.

Mr. Stuart's laugh cleared the sorrowful atmosphere of the study as though by magic. Ruth and Barbara smiled through their tears. They were now so sure that all would soon be well!

"It seems to me, William, that all this is 'much ado about nothing,'" Mr. Stuart declared. "Of course, I can see that the situation would have been pretty serious if poor Harriet had been deceived into giving up the real documents. But Bab and Ruth have saved the day! There is no harm done now. You even know the names of the spies. There is only one thing for us to consider at present, and that is—where is Harriet?"

"Yes, Father," Ruth pleaded. "Do find Harriet."

"The child was foolish, and she did wrong, of course," Mr. Stuart went on. "But, as Ruth tells me Harriet did not know the real papers were exchanged for false ones, she probably thinks she has disgraced you and she is too frightened to come home. You must take steps to find her at once, and to let her know you forgive her. It is a pity to lose any time."

Mr. Hamlin was silent. "I cannot forgive Harriet," he replied. "But, of course, she must be brought home at once."

"Nonsense!" Mr. Stuart continued. "Summon your servants and have some one telephone to Harriet's friends. She has probably gone to one of them. Tell the child that Sallie and I are here and wish to see her. But where are my other 'Automobile Girls,' Mollie and Grace?"

"Upstairs, Father," Ruth answered happily. "Come and see them. I want to telephone for Harriet. I think she will come home for me."

"Show your aunt and father to their rooms, Ruth," Mr. Hamlin begged. "I must wait here until a messenger arrives from the newspaper, which in some way has learned the story of our misfortune. And even they do not know that the stolen papers were valueless. I must explain matters to them."

"A man of your influence can keep any mention of this affair out of the newspapers," Mr. Stuart argued heartily. "So the storm will have blown over by to-morrow. And I believe you will be able to punish the two schemers who have tried to betray your daughter and disgrace my Barbara, without having Harriet's name brought into this affair."

For the first time, Mr. Hamlin lifted his head and nodded briefly. "Yes, I can attend to them," he declared in the quiet fashion that showed him to be a man of power. "It is best, for the sake of the country, that the scandal be nipped in the bud. I alone know what was in these state papers that Mrs. Wilson and Peter Dillon were hired to steal. So I alone know to whom they would be valuable. There would be an international difficulty if I should expose the real promoter of the theft. Peter Dillon shall be dismissed from his Embassy. Mrs. Wilson will find it wiser to leave Washington, and never to return here again. I will spare the woman as much as I can for the sake of her son, Elmer, who is a fine fellow. Ruth, dear, do telephone to Harriet's friends. Your father is right. We must find my daughter at once."

Miss Sallie, Mr. Stuart and Ruth started to leave the room. Bab rose to follow them.

"Miss Thurston, don't go for a minute," Mr. Hamlin said. "I wish to beg your pardon. Will you forgive a most unhappy man? Of course I see, now, that I had no right to suspect you without giving you a chance to defend yourself. I can only say that I was deceived, as well as Harriet. The whole plot is plain to me now. Harriet was to be terrified into not betraying her own part in the theft, so she would never dare reveal the names of Mrs. Wilson or Peter Dillon. I, with my mind poisoned against you, would have sought blindly to fasten the crime on you. I regard my office as Assistant Secretary of State as a sacred trust. If the papers entrusted to my keeping had been delivered into the hands of the enemies of my country, through my own daughter's folly, I should never have lifted my head again, I cannot say—I have no words to express—what I owe to you and Ruth. But how do you think a newspaper man could have unearthed this plot? It seems incredible, when you consider how stealthily Peter Dillon and Mrs. Wilson have worked. A man—"

"I don't think a man did unearth it," Bab replied. Just then the bell rang again.

The next moment the door opened, and the butler announced: "Miss Marjorie Moore!" The newspaper girl gave Bab a friendly smile; then she turned coldly to Mr. William Hamlin.

"Miss Moore!" Mr. Hamlin exclaimed in surprise and in anger. "I wish to see a man from your newspaper. What I have to say cannot possibly concern you."

"I think it does, Mr. Hamlin," Miss Moore repeated calmly. "One of the editors from my paper has come here with me. He is waiting in the hall. But it was I who discovered the theft of your state documents. I have been expecting mischief for some time. I am sorry for you, of course—very sorry, but I have all the facts of the case, and as no one else knows of it, it will be a great scoop for me in the morning."

"Your newspaper will not publish the story at all, Miss Moore," Mr. Hamlin rejoined, when he had recovered from his astonishment at Miss Moore's appearance. "The stolen papers were not of the least value. Will you explain to Miss Moore exactly what occurred, Miss Thurston?" Mr.

Hamlin concluded.

When Bab told the story of how she and Ruth had made their lightning substitution of the papers, Marjorie Moore gave a gasp of surprise.

"Good for you, Miss Thurston!" she returned. "I knew you were clever, as well as the right sort, the first time I saw you. So I had gotten hold of the whole story of the theft except, the most important point—the exchange of the papers. It spoils my story as sensational political news. But," Miss Moore laughed, "it makes a perfectly great personal story, because it has such a funny side to it: 'Foiled by the "Automobile Girls"!' 'The Assistant Secretary of State's Daughter!'" Miss Moore stopped, ashamed of her cruelty when she saw Mr. Hamlin's face. But he did not speak.

It was Bab who exclaimed: "Oh, Miss Moore, you are not going to betray Harriet, are you? Poor Harriet thought it was all a joke. She did not know the papers were valuable. It would be too cruel to spread this story abroad. It might ruin Harriet's reputation."

Marjorie Moore made no answer.

"You heard Miss Thurston," Mr. Hamlin interposed. "Surely you will grant our request."

"Mr. Hamlin," Marjorie Moore protested, "I am dreadfully sorry for you. I told you so, but I am going to have this story published in the morning. It is too good to keep and I have worked dreadfully hard on it. Indeed, I almost lost my life because of it. I knew it was Peter Dillon who struck me down on the White House lawn the night of the reception. But I said nothing because I knew that, if I made trouble, I would have been put off the scent of the story somehow. I tried to see Miss Thurston alone, that evening, to warn her that Mrs. Wilson and Peter Dillon were going to try to fasten their crime on her. I am obliged to be frank with you, Mr. Hamlin. I will stick to the facts as you have told them to me, but a full account of the attempted theft will be published in the morning's 'News.'"

"Call the man who is with you, Miss Moore; I prefer to talk with him," Mr. Hamlin commanded. "You do not seem to realize the gravity of what you intend to do. It will be a mistake for your newspaper to make an enemy of a man in my official position."

Mr. Hamlin talked for some time to one of the editors of the Washington "News." He entreated, threatened and finally made an appeal to him to save his daughter and himself by not making the story public.

"I am afraid we shall have to let the story go, Miss Moore," the editor remarked regretfully. "It was a fine piece of news, but we don't wish to make things too hard for Mr. Hamlin." The man turned to go.

"Mr. Hughes," Marjorie Moore announced, speaking to her editor, "if you do not intend to use this story, which I have worked on so long, in your paper, I warn you, right now, that I shall simply sell it to some other newspaper and take the consequences. All the papers will not be so careful of Mr. Hamlin's feelings."

"Oh, Miss Moore, you would not be so cruel!" Bab cried.

Marjorie Moore turned suddenly on Barbara; "Why shouldn't I?" she returned. "Both Harriet Hamlin and Peter Dillon have been hateful and insolent to me ever since I have been making my living in Washington. I told you I meant to get even with them some day. Well, this is my chance, and I intend to take it. Good-bye; there is no reason for me to stay here any longer."

"Mr. Hamlin, if Miss Moore insists on selling her story on the outside, I cannot see how we would benefit you by failing to print the story," the editor added.

"Very well," Mr. Hamlin returned coldly. But he sank back into his chair and covered his face with his hands. Harriet's reputation was ruined, for no one would believe she had not tried deliberately to sell her father's honor.

But Bab resolved to appeal once more to the newspaper girl. She ran to Marjorie Moore and put her arm about the newspaper girl's waist to detain her. She talked to her in her most winning fashion, with her brown eyes glowing with feeling and her lips trembling with eagerness.

The tears came to Marjorie Moore's eyes as she listened to Bab's pleading for Harriet. But she still obstinately shook her head.

Some one came running down the stairs and Ruth entered the study without heeding the strangers in it.

"Uncle!" she exclaimed in a terrified voice, "Harriet cannot be found! We have telephoned everywhere for her. No one has seen her or knows anything about her. What shall we do? It is midnight!"

Mr. Hamlin followed Ruth quickly out of the room, forgetting every other consideration in his fear for his daughter. He looked broken and old. Was Harriet in some worse peril?

As Marjorie Moore saw Mr. Hamlin go, she turned swiftly to Barbara and kissed her. "It's all right, dear," she said. "You were right. Revenge is too little and too mean. Mr. Hughes has said he will not publish the story, and I shall not sell it anywhere else. Indeed, I promise that what I know shall never be spoken of outside this room. Good night." Before Barbara could thank her she was gone.

CHAPTER XXIII

All night long diligent search was made for Harriet Hamlin, but no word was heard of her. The "Automobile Girls" telephoned her dearest friends. Mr. Hamlin and Mr. Stuart tramped from one hotel to the other. None of the Hamlin household closed their eyes that night.

"It has been my fault, Robert," Mr. Hamlin admitted, as he and his brother-in-law returned home in the gray dawn of the morning, hoping vainly to hear that Harriet had returned. "My child has gotten into debt and she has been afraid to confess her mistake to me. Her little friend, Mollie, told me the story. Mollie believes that Mrs. Wilson and Peter Dillon tempted Harriet by offering to lend her money. And so she agreed to aid them in what she thought was their 'joke.' I have seen, lately, that Harriet has been so worried she hardly knew what she was doing. Yet, when my poor child tried to confess her fault to me, I would not let her go on. My harshness and lack of sympathy have driven her to—I know not what. Oh, Robert, what shall I do? She is the one joy of my life!"

Mr. Stuart did not try to deny Mr. Hamlin's judgment of himself. He knew Mr. Hamlin had been too severe with his daughter. If only Harriet could be found she and her father would be closer friends after this experience. Mr. Stuart realized fully what danger Harriet was in with her unusual beauty, with no mother and with a father who did not understand her.

"Harriet has done very wrong," Mr. Hamlin added slowly. It was hard, indeed, for a man of his nature to forgive. "But I shall not reproach her when she comes back to me," he said quickly. The fear that Harriet might never return to him at all struck a sudden chill to his soul.

"The child has done wrong, William, I admit it," returned good-natured Mr. Stuart. "She has been headstrong and foolish. But we have done worse things in our day, remember."

"I will remember," Mr. Hamlin answered drearily, as he shut himself up in his room.

Mr. Hamlin would not come down to breakfast. There was still no news of Harriet. While dear, comfortable Aunt Sallie and the "Automobile Girls" were seated around the table, making a pretense of eating, there came a ring at the front door bell.

Ruth jumped up and ran out into the hall. Then followed several moments of awful suspense. Ruth came back slowly, not with Harriet, but with a note in her hand. She opened it with shaking fingers, for she recognized Harriet's handwriting in the address.

The note read: "Dearest Ruth, I shall never come home again. I have disgraced my father and myself. I would not listen to you and Bab, and now I know the worst. Mrs. Wilson and Peter Dillon were villains and I was only a foolish dupe. I spent the night in a boarding house with an old friend of my mother's." Ruth stopped reading. Her voice sank so low it was almost impossible to hear her. She had not noticed that her uncle was standing just outside the door, listening, with white lips.

"I don't know what else to do," Harriet's note continued, when Ruth had strength to go on. "So early this morning I telegraphed to Charlie Meyers. When you receive this note, I shall be married to him. Ask my father to forgive me, for I shall never see him again. Your heart-broken cousin, Harriet."

"Absurd child!" Miss Sallie ejaculated, trying to hide her tears. But Mr. Stuart stepped to Mr. Hamlin's side as he entered the room, looking conscience-stricken and miserable.

Poor Harriet was paying for her folly with a life-time of wretchedness. She was to marry a man she did not love; and her friends were powerless to save her.

Mollie slipped quietly away from the table. No one tried to stop her. Every one thought Mollie was overcome, because she had been especially devoted to Harriet.

"Won't you try to find Mr. Meyers, Uncle?" Ruth pleaded. "It may not be too late to prevent Harriet's marriage. Oh, do try to find her. She does not care for Charlie Meyers in the least. She is only marrying him because she is so wretched she does not know what to do."

Mr. Stuart was already getting into his coat and hat. Mr. Hamlin was not far behind him. The two men were just going out the front door, when a cry from Mollie interrupted them. The three girls rushed into the hall, not knowing what Mollie's cry meant. But when they saw the little golden haired girl, who sympathized the most deeply with Harriet in her trouble, because of her own recent acquaintance with debt, the "Automobile Girls" knew at once that all was well!

"Oh, Mr. Hamlin! Oh, Mr. Stuart! Do wait until I get my breath," Mollie begged. "Dear, darling Harriet is all right. She will come home if her father will come for her. I telephoned to Mr. Meyers and he declares Harriet is safe with his aunt. He says, of course, he is not such a cad as to marry Harriet when she is so miserable and frightened. He went to the boarding house for her, then took her to his aunt's home. Mr. Meyers was on his way here to see Mr. Hamlin."

Two hours later, Harriet was at home again and in bed, suffering from nervous shock. But her father's forgiveness, his sympathy, his reassuring words, and above all, the thought that by the ruse of Bab, she had been mercifully saved from the deep disgrace that had shadowed her life, soon restored her to her normal spirits. There was a speedy investigation by the State Department—the result of which was that Mrs. Wilson disappeared from Washington society. Her son Elmer reported that his mother had grown tired of Washington and was living in New England. As for Peter Dillon, his connection with the Russian Embassy was severed at once. No one knew where he went.

*   *   *   *   *

"The President would like to see the 'Automobile Girls' at the White House to-day at half past twelve o'clock," Mr. William Hamlin announced a few mornings later, looking up from his paper to smile first at his daughter and then at the group of happy faces about his breakfast table, which included Miss Sallie Stuart and Mr. Robert Stuart.

Harriet was looking very pale. She had been ill for two days after her unhappy experience.

"What on earth do you mean, Mr. Hamlin?" inquired Grace Carter anxiously, turning to their host.

The other girls smiled, thinking Mr. Hamlin was joking, he had been in such different spirits since Harriet's return home.

"I mean what I say," Mr. Hamlin returned gravely. "The President wishes to see the 'Automobile Girls' in order to thank them for their service to their country." Mr. Hamlin allowed an earnest note to creep into his voice. "The story has not been made public. But I myself told the

President of my narrow escape from disgrace, and he desires personally to thank the young girls who saved us. I told him that he might rely on your respecting his invitation."

"Oh, but we can't go, Mr. Hamlin," Mollie expostulated. "Grace and I had nothing to do with saving the papers. It was only Ruth and Bab!"

"It is most unusual to decline an invitation from the President, Mollie," Mr. Hamlin continued. "Only a death in the family is regarded as a reasonable excuse. Now the President most distinctly stated that he desired a visit from the 'Automobile Girls'!"

"United we stand, divided we fall!" Ruth announced. "Bab and I will not stir a single step without Grace and Mollie."

"There is one other person who ought to be included in this visit to the President," Harriet added, shyly.

"Whom do you mean, my child?" Mr. Hamlin queried.

Harriet hung her proud little head. "I mean Marjorie Moore, Father. I think she did as much as any one by keeping the story out of the papers when it would have meant so much for her to have published it."

"Good for Harriet!" Ruth murmured under her breath.

"I did not neglect to tell the President of Miss Moore's part in the affair, Daughter," Mr. Hamlin rejoined. "But I am glad you spoke of it. I shall certainly see that she is included in the invitation."

Promptly at twelve o'clock the "Automobile Girls" set out for the White House in the care of their old and faithful friend, Mr. A. Bubble. On the way there they picked up Marjorie Moore, who had now become their staunch friend.

The girls were greatly excited over their second visit to the White House. It was, of course, very unlike their first, since to-day they were to be the special guests of the President. On the evening of the Presidential reception they had been merely included among several hundred callers.

Ruth sent in Mr. Hamlin's card with theirs, in order to explain whose visitors they were. The five girls were immediately shown into a small room, which the President used for seeing his friends when he desired a greater privacy than was possible in the large state reception rooms.

The girls sat waiting the appearance of the President, each one a little more nervous than the other.

"What shall we say, Bab?" Mollie whispered to her sister.

"Goodness knows, child!" Bab just had time to answer, when a servant bowed ceremoniously. A man entered the room quickly and walked from one girl to the other, shaking hands with each one in turn.

"I am very glad to meet you," he declared affably. "Mr. Hamlin tells me you were able to do him a service, and through him to your country, which it is also my privilege to serve. I thank you." The President bowed ceremoniously. "It was a pretty trick you played on our enemies. Strategy is sometimes better than war, and a woman's wits than a man's fists." Then the President turned cordially to Marjorie Moore.

"Miss Moore, it gives me pleasure to say a word of appreciation to you. Your act in withholding this information from the public rather than to sell it and make a personal gain by it, was a thoroughly patriotic act, and I wish you to know that I value your service."

"Thank you, Mr. President," replied Miss Moore, blushing deeply.

The President's wife now entered the sitting-room with several other guests and members of her family. When luncheon was announced, the President of the United States offered his arm to Barbara Thurston.

The "Automobile Girls" are not likely to forget their luncheon with the President, his family and a few intimate friends. The girls were frightened at first; but, being simple and natural, they soon ceased to think of themselves. They were too much interested in what they saw and heard around them.

The President talked to Ruth, who sat on his left, about automobiles. He was interested to hear of the travels of Mr. A. Bubble, and seemed to know a great deal about motor cars. But, after a while, as the girls heard him converse with three distinguished men who sat at his table, one an engineer, the other a judge, and the third an artist, the "Automobile Girls" decided wisely that the President knew almost everything that was worth knowing.

*   *   *   *   *

"Children," said Mr. Stuart that night, when the girls could tell no more of their day's experience, "it seems to me that it is about time for you to be going home." Mr. Stuart and Aunt Sallie were in the Hamlin drawing-room with the "Automobile Girls." Mr. Hamlin and Harriet had gone for a short walk. It was now their custom to walk together each evening after dinner, since it gave them a little opportunity for a confidential talk.

"You girls have had to-day the very happiest opportunity that falls to the lot of any visitor in Washington," Mr. Stuart continued. "You have had a private interview with the President and have been entertained by him at the Executive Mansion. I have no doubt you have also seen all the sights of Washington in the last few weeks. So homeward-bound must be our next forward move!"

"Oh, Father," cried Ruth regretfully, her face clouding as she looked at her beloved automobile friends. How long before she should see them again?

The same thought clouded the bright faces of Mollie, Grace and Bab.

"We have hardly seen you at all, Miss Sallie," Grace lamented, taking Miss Sarah Stuart's plump, white hand in her own. "We have been the centre of so much excitement ever since you arrived in Washington."

"Must we go, Father?" Ruth entreated.

"I am afraid we must, Daughter," Mr. Stuart answered, with a half anxious and half cheerful twinkle in his eye.

"Then it's Chicago for me!" sighed Ruth.

"And Kingsbridge for the rest of us!" echoed the other three girls.

"Ruth cannot very well travel home alone," Mr. Stuart remonstrated, looking first at Barbara, then at Mollie and Grace, and winking solemnly at Miss Sallie.

"Don't tease the child, Robert," Miss Sallie remonstrated.

"Aren't you and Aunt Sallie going home with me, Father?" Ruth queried, too much surprised for further questioning.

"No, Ruth," Mr. Stuart declared. "You seem to have concluded to return to Chicago. But your Aunt Sallie and I are on our way to Kingsbridge, New Jersey, to pay a visit to Mrs. Mollie Thurston at Laurel Cottage. Mrs. Thurston wrote inviting us to visit her before we returned to the West. But, of course, if you do not wish to go with us, Daughter—."

Mr. Stuart had no chance to speak again. For the four girls surrounded him, plying him with questions, with exclamations. They were all laughing and talking at once.

"It's too good to be true, Father!" cried Ruth.

CHAPTER XXIV

Mrs. Thurston stood on the front porch of her little cottage, looking out in the gathering dusk. Back of her the lights twinkled gayly. A big wood fire crackled in the sitting-room and shone through the soft muslin curtains. A small maid was busily setting the table for supper in the dinning room, and there was a delicious smell of freshly baked rolls coming through the kitchen door. On the table stood a great dish of golden honey and a pitcher of rich milk. Mrs. Thurston had not forgotten, in two years, the favorite supper of her friend, Robert Stuart.

It was a cold night, but she could not wait indoors. She had gathered up a warm woolen shawl of a delicate lavender shade, and wrapped it about her head and shoulders, looking not unlike the gracious spirit of an Autumn twilight as she lingered to welcome the travelers home. She was thinking of all that had happened since the day that Bab had stopped Ruth's runaway horses. She was recalling how much Mr. Stuart had done for her little girls in the past two years. "He could not have been kinder to Mollie and Barbara, if they had been his own daughters," thought pretty Mrs. Thurston, with a blush.

But did she not hear the ever-welcome sound of a friendly voice? Was not Mr. Bubble calling to her out of the darkness? Surely enough his two great shining eyes now appeared at the well-known turn in the road. A few moments later Mrs. Thurston was being tempestuously embraced by the "Automobile Girls."

"Do let me speak to Miss Stuart, children," Mrs. Thurston entreated, trying to extricate herself from four pairs of girlish arms.

"Come in, Miss Stuart," she laughed. "I hope you are not tired from your journey. I cannot tell you what pleasure it gives me to see you and Mr. Stuart once more."

Mr. Stuart gave Mrs. Thurston's hand a little longer pressure than was absolutely necessary. Mrs. Thurston blushed and finally drew her hand away.

"Look after Mr. Stuart, dear," she said to Bab. "He is to have the guest chamber upstairs. I want to show Miss Stuart to her room. I am sorry, Ruth, our little home is too small to give you a room to yourself. You will have to be happy with Mollie and Bab. Grace you are to stay to supper with us. Your father will come for you after supper. I had to beg awfully hard, but he finally consented to let you remain with us. Our little reunion would not be complete without you."

Mrs. Thurston took Miss Sallie into a charming room which she had lately renovated for her guest. It was papered in Miss Stuart's favorite lavender paper, had lavender curtains at the windows, and a bright wood fire in the grate.

"I hope you will be comfortable, Miss Stuart," said little Mrs. Thurston, who stood slightly in awe of stately and elegant Miss Sallie.

For answer Miss Sallie smiled and looked searchingly at Mrs. Thurston.

"Is there any question you wish to ask me?" Mrs. Thurston inquired, flushing slightly at Miss Stuart's peculiar expression.

"Oh, no," smiled Miss Sallie. "Oh, no, I have no question to ask you!"

It was seven o'clock when the party sat down to supper, and after nine when they finally rose.

They stopped then only because Squire Carter arrived and demanded his daughter, Grace, whom he had to carry off, as he and her mother could bear to be parted from their child no longer.

Miss Sallie asked to be excused, soon after supper, as she was tired from her trip. "I think the 'Automobile Girls' had better go to bed, too," she suggested. Then Miss Sallie flushed. For she was so accustomed to telling her girls what they ought to do that she forgot it was no longer her privilege to advise Bab and Mollie when they were in their mother's house.

Bab insisted on running out to their little stable to see if her beloved horse, "Beauty," were safe and sound. And, of course, Ruth and Mollie went with her. But not long afterwards, the three girls retired to their room to talk until they fell asleep, too worn out for further conversation.

"I am not tired, Mrs. Thurston, are you?" Mr. Stuart asked. "If you don't mind, won't you sit and talk to me for a little while before this cozy open fire? We never have a chance to say much to each other before our talkative daughters. How charming the little cottage looks to-night! It is like a second home."

Mrs. Thurston smiled happily. "It makes me very happy to have you and Ruth feel so. I hope you will always feel at home here. I wish I could do something in return for all the kindness you have shown to my two little girls."

Mr. Stuart did not reply at once. He seemed to be thinking so deeply that

Mrs. Thurston did not like to go on talking.

"Mrs. Thurston," Mr. Stuart spoke slowly, "why would you not come to my house in Chicago to make us a visit when I asked you, nearly a year ago?"

Mrs. Thurston hesitated. "I told you my reasons then, Mr. Stuart. It was quite impossible. But it has been so long I have almost forgotten why I had to refuse."

"It was after our trip in the private car with our friends, the fall before, you remember, Mrs. Thurston. But I know why you would not come to my home," Mr. Stuart answered, smiling. "You were willing to accept my hospitality for your daughters, but you would not accept it for yourself. Am I not right?"

"Yes," Mrs. Thurston faltered. "I thought it would not be best."

"I am sorry," Mr. Stuart said sadly. "Because I want to do a great deal more than ask you to come to visit me in Chicago. I wish you to come to live there as my wife."

Mrs. Thurston's reply was so low it could hardly be heard. But Mr. Stuart evidently understood it and found it satisfactory.

A few moments later Mrs. Thurston murmured, "I don't believe that Ruth and your sister Sallie will be pleased."

"Ruth will be the happiest girl in the world!" Mr. Stuart retorted. "Poor child, she has longed for sisters all her life. Now she is going to have the two she loves best in the world. As for Sallie—." Here Mr. Stuart hesitated. He thought Miss Sallie did not dream of his affection for the little widow, and he was not at all sure how she would receive the news. "As for Sallie," he continued stoutly, "I am sure Sallie wishes my happiness more than anything else and she will be glad when she hears that I can find it only through you."

Mrs. Thurston shook her head. "I can only consent to our marriage," she returned, "if my girls and yours are really happy in our choice and if your sister is willing to give us her blessing."

* * * * *

"Oh, Aunt Sallie, dear, please are you awake?" Ruth cried at half-past seven the next morning, tapping gently on Miss Stuart's door.

Ruth had been awakened by her father at a little after six that morning and carried off to his bedroom in her dressing-gown, to sit curled up on her father's bed, while he made his confession to her.

Ruth had listened silently at first with her head turned away. Once her father thought she was crying. But when she turned toward him her eyes were shining with happy tears. Ruth never thought of being jealous, or that her adored father would love her any less. She only thought, first, of his happiness and next of her own.

Mr. Stuart would not let Ruth go until, with her arms about his neck and her cheek pressed to his, she begged him to let her be the messenger to Barbara, Mollie and Aunt Sallie.

"You will be careful when you break the news to your aunt," Mr. Stuart entreated. "I should have given her some warning in regard to my feelings for Mrs. Thurston. I fear the news will be an entire surprise to her."

Ruth wondered what she should say first.

"Come in, dear," Miss Sallie answered placidly in reply to Ruth's knock. Miss Stuart was sitting up in bed with a pale lavender silk dressing sacque over her lace and muslin gown.

"I suppose," Miss Sallie continued calmly, "that you have come to tell me that your father is going to marry Mrs. Thurston."

"Aunt Sallie," gasped Ruth, "are you a wizard?"

"No," said Miss Stuart, "I am a woman. Why, child, I have seen this thing coming ever since we first left Robert Stuart here in Kingsbridge when I took you girls off to Newport. Are you pleased, child?" Miss Sallie inquired, a little wistfully.

"Gladder than anything, if you are, Aunt Sallie," Ruth replied. "But Father told me to come to ask you how you felt. He says Mrs. Thurston won't marry him unless we all consent."

"Nonsense!" returned Miss Stuart in her accustomed fashion. "Of course I am glad to have Robert happy. Mrs. Thurston is a dear little woman. Only," dignified Miss Sallie choked with a tiny sob in her voice, "I can't give you up, Ruth, dear." And Miss Stuart and her beloved niece shed a few comfortable tears in each other's arms.

"I never, never will care for any one as I do for you, Aunt Sallie," Ruth protested. "And aren't you Chaperon Extraordinary and Ministering Angel Plentipotentiary to the 'Automobile Girls'? The other girls care for you almost as much as I do. I wonder if Mrs. Thurston has told Bab and Mollie. Do you think they will be glad to have me for a sister?"

"Fix my hair, Ruth, and don't be absurd," Miss Sallie rejoined, returning to her former severe manner, which no longer alarmed any one of the "Automobile Girls." "It is wonderful to me how I have learned to do without a maid while I have been traveling about the world with you children."

The winter sunshine poured into the breakfast room of Laurel Cottage. The canary sang rapturously in his golden cage. He rejoiced at the sound of voices and the cheerful sounds in the house.

Bab and Mollie were helping to set the breakfast table, when Ruth joined them. Neither girl said anything except to ask Ruth why she had slipped out of their room so early.

Ruth's heart sank. After all, then, Barbara and Mollie were not pleased. They did not care for her enough to be happy in this closer bond between them.

Mrs. Thurston kissed Ruth shyly, but she made no mention of anything unusual. And when Mr. Stuart came in to breakfast he looked as embarrassed and uncomfortable as a boy. There was a constraint over the little party at breakfast that had not been there the night before.

Unexpectedly the door opened. Into the room came Grace Carter with a big bunch of white roses in her hand. "I just had to come early," she declared simply. "I wanted to find out." Grace thrust the flowers upon Mrs. Thurston.

"Come here to me, Grace," Miss Sallie commanded. "You are a girl after my own heart. Robert, Mrs. Thurston, I congratulate you and I wish you joy with my whole heart."

Barbara and Mollie gazed at each other in stupefied silence. What did it all mean?

Mrs. Thurston blushed like a girl over her roses. "Miss Stuart, I never dreamed you could have heard so soon. I have not yet told Barbara and Mollie."

"Told us what?" Bab demanded in her emphatic fashion. Then Ruth's heart was light again.

But Bab did not wait to be answered. She suddenly guessed the truth. Now she knew why Ruth's manner had changed so quickly a short time before. She ran round the table, upsetting her chair in her rush. And before she said a word either to her mother or to Mr. Stuart, she flung her arms about Ruth and whispered: "Our wish has come true, Ruth, darling! We are sisters as well as best friends."

Then Bab congratulated her mother and Mr. Stuart in a much more dignified fashion.

"When is it to be, Father?" Ruth queried.

Mr. Stuart looked at Mrs. Thurston. "In the spring," she faltered.

"Then we will all go away together and have a happy summer, somewhere,"

Mr. Stuart asserted, smiling on the faces of his dear ones.

"We shall do no such thing, Robert Stuart," Miss Sallie interposed firmly. "You shall have your honeymoon alone. I intend to take my 'Automobile Girls' some place where we have never been before. Will you go with me, children?"

"Yes," chorused the four girls. "Aunt Sallie and the 'Automobile Girls' forever."

Made in the USA
Lexington, KY
21 February 2018